THE NOOSE WAS AROUND CORT'S NECK, AND THE CHAIR WAS DOWN TO ONE LEG.

Ellen heard the chair creak and sway as Cort balanced his weight. She saw the hard resolve on his face and wondered if he'd accept death before compromise.

"Go ahead, Herod. You know I'm past begging," he said.

"This is your last chance, Cort." Herod shrugged. "It's yes or no. It's kill or be killed. It's hope or maggot bait." Slowly Herod settled the Peacemaker's sights on the fourth chair leg, waiting for an answer.

Hardly aware that she was standing, let alone speaking out, Ellen murmured into the vast silence, "Put my name up."

Every eye in the room turned to look at her. Horace stammered, "There is no women allowed in the quick draw. It's a rule."

Herod looked at her with new interest. He had no recollection of her as he lazily undressed her with his eyes, liking what he saw.

Cort looked at her in a different way. He could only hope for the best.

"There are no rules that prohibit ladies from entering the contest. It's just that females can't shoot for shit," Herod growled. Turning back toward Cort, he said heatedly, "I'm tired of this. I'll make up your mind for you."

Again the golden six-gun arced downward, and as the hammer fell, the fourth chair leg shattered.

She felt her hand drop to the Colt .44 as if she had nothing to do with it, as if she were a bystander watching a strongly built woman neatly, with no wasted motion, clearing leather, pointing the weapon, the heel of her left hand fanning off three shots so fast they sounded like one. . . .

Books by Jack Curtis

The Quick and the Dead* (Novelization)
The Quiet Cowboy*
Pepper Tree Rider
The Mark of Cain*
Cut and Branded*
Wild River Massacre*
The Fight for San Bernardo*
Blood to Burn*
Paradise Valley*
The Jury on Smoky Hill*
Blood Cut*
Texas Rules*
The Sheriff Kill*
Red Knife Valley
Eagles Over Big Sur
Banjo
Klootchman

*Published by POCKET BOOKS

THE QUICK AND THE DEAD

A Novel by JACK CURTIS
Based on a Screenplay by SIMON MOORE

POCKET BOOKS
New York   London   Toronto   Sydney   Tokyo   Singapore

This book is a work of fiction. Names, characters, places and incidents are products of the author's imagination or are used fictitiously. Any resemblance to actual events or locales or persons, living or dead, is entirely coincidental.

Portions of the article "Writing Westerns" by Jim Cole, copyright © 1991 by *Coast Weekly,* Monterey, California, are printed by permission.

An *Original* Publication of POCKET BOOKS

POCKET BOOKS, a division of Simon & Schuster Inc.
1230 Avenue of the Americas, New York, NY 10020

ISBN: 0-671-51898-4

First Pocket Books printing March 1995

10 9 8 7 6 5 4 3 2 1

POCKET and colophon are registered trademarks of Simon & Schuster Inc.

Printed in the U.S.A.

For Doug Grad

Iron sharpeneth iron;
so a man sharpeneth
the countenance of his friend.

—*Book of Proverbs*

The third day He rose from the dead:
He ascended into heaven, and sitteth
on the right hand of God the Father
Almighty: From thence He shall come to
judge the quick and the dead.

—Apostle's Creed
Book of Common Prayer

on the following sound.

Staring out into the dusk, she felt that it was a

THE QUICK AND THE DEAD

Prologue

THUNDER. FROM ACROSS THE RIVER THUNDER CAME rolling. . . .

Starting as a single trading post, Redemption had grown into a respectable hamlet of nearly twenty businesses run by family-loving citizens who believed hard work would create wealth, that cleanliness was next to godliness, and that a lawful community would attract more settlers, more business, more prosperity.

The sky was clear as a bluebird's eye, the day was fair. . . .

Accordingly, the townsfolk built the City Hall on the southwest corner of the town square, complete with space for the volunteer fire brigade's red and gold pump and hose rig on the bottom floor, a courtroom and city offices on the second floor, and a grand clock tower on top which could be seen and heard miles away.

Yet the thunder came rolling on. . . .

Across from the clock tower stood the red brick Bank of Redemption. The other corners were taken up by Whiteside's Mercantile and the Square Deal Hardware. Along Main Street, built of milled lumber painted white, were the two-story rooming house with its veranda and balcony, called the Stockman's Rest; Dr. Wallace's office; the false-fronted carpentry shop; and a harness shop. Opposite them, next to the clock tower, stood the jail and Marshal McKenzie's office.

Morning sunbeams warmed the street and larks sang. . . .

The grand cream-colored limestone church blocked off Main Street just up from the town square. How the church happened to make a T of Main Street no one remembered, but it seemed proper that all roads should lead to the House of the Lord.

A cavalcade of iron-shod hooves came pounding on. . . .

The city fathers planted and watered sweet clover in the street to keep the dust down and freshen the air, and despite the horses and wagons, the street stayed green, filled with the buzzing of honey bees, and was even edible.

Like distant artillery or a band of highwaymen swarming toward the hapless village, the unearthly rumbling came on. . . .

There were no saloons in Redemption, no dance halls, no casinos or card rooms, no red-light district, no zone of tolerance, no billiard parlors, and only one prisoner in Marshal McKenzie's jail, an outsider named John Herod.

Hoofbeats, muffled by the shallow river crossing, rose and fell, and still the thunder came rolling. . . .

Quiet-mannered, Marshal McKenzie picked up the empty white enameled bowl from the floor and looked in at his prisoner.

"Have aplenty?" he asked.

"My compliments, Marshal," the prisoner said, nodding. "Your mush is superior to most."

Herod's voice was deep and melodious, a thick, muddy drawl that evoked the indolent power of the deep South.

"Thank you, Mr. Herod." The Marshal smiled. "Too bad you'll be missing dinner. I'm cooking up a batch of Chicken Maryland."

"Why will I miss it?" Herod asked, a frown showing in the tight movement of his wide eyebrows. As tall as the marshal, he was built of heavier bone, which showed especially in the bulkiness of his shoulders.

He wore striped worsted trousers that reached the ankles of his calfskin boots. The vest was of embroidered silk, and his tailored gray frock coat looked new. Pacing back and forth in the small cell, his gold inlaid spurs whirred like an aroused rattlesnake.

"I'm takin' you on over to Tucson on the next stage," the marshal said. "They want you first."

3

Gathering a bouquet of white clover blossoms from the street, the marshal's daughter, seven-year-old Ellen McKenzie, idly sang,

> "Jesus loves me
> This I know
> For the Bible tells me so . . ."

Golden-haired, she was tall and gawky for her age, and in that way resembled her mother, who had died in the cholera epidemic two years before.

Halfway between her father's office and Doc Wallace's across the broad street, she heard the distant rumble. Looking to the east, she saw no storm clouds, and she resumed her carefree quest for clover blossoms which she intended to give to her friend, the doctor.

And the rumbling thunder of horses' hooves drummed up the river bluff and came on like Jehovah's wrath condemning and crushing the sweet green grass of home. . . .

Herod paused a moment to listen to the approaching rumble coming through the barred window, then smiled and said, "I've always wanted my own town, Marshal. I reckon I'll stay, and you'll be leaving."

"It won't be that way, Herod." McKenzie shook his head. "Even if they hang you two or three times over there, they still won't be satisfied."

"I'm innocent, Marshal." Herod's heavy features, crossed by a black, closely clipped mustache, revealed a sense of merriment. "I was a peaceful wayfarer asleep in your hotel when you arrested me."

"With a man of your reputation, Mr. Herod, I wouldn't do it any other way." The marshal smiled.

"I'm a simple traveler, sir. A gentleman from the sovereign state of Mississippi."

"A Mississippi gentleman crossed on an alligator and mixed in with some curly wolf," the marshal said, and added, "Sounds like thunder, don't it?"

"It's likely there'll be a storm, Marshal." Herod permitted a smile to touch his wide lips, but his eyes, hidden deep under his overhanging brow, were cold and contemptuous.

"A shower'd be good for the clover," the marshal said agreeably. "I reckon you're all packed and ready to go?"

"You shouldn't make fun of a helpless prisoner, Marshal," Herod said gravely. "There may come a day when you'll regret it."

Outside, Ellen ignored the thunder rising and rolling toward the town as she wandered about the placid street.

Mr. Murdock, the banker, stepped out on the porch of the bank, listening uncertainly. Mr. Whiteside poked his head warily out of the front door of the mercantile. The massing of hoofbeats coming with a measured sureness of purpose was not new to him. He had come west from Lawrence, Kansas, after Quantrill's Raiders had burned his store and his house. He knew that unforgettable thunder for what it was.

"Lock up and run for it, Mr. Murdock," he yelled, and retreated inside his darkened store, pausing only to wedge the two-by-fours into its hangers to bar the door, then dashing in a panic out the back way to the alley.

Murdock stared questioningly at the closed door of the mercantile and tried to understand what Whiteside was yelling about.

Yes, riders were coming up from the river, but they could be a company of cavalry passing through. Likely they would stop for supplies. Maybe some of them would see what a nice town they had and remember it later on when their enlistments were up.

Any strangers passing by ought to be seen as an opportunity for new growth. It was definitely wrong-headedness to close the door in their faces.

Shaking his head in disapproval, Murdock thought Redemption was a good Christian town, better than most, mainly because its people were friendly to strangers, didn't overcharge, and kept everything clean and bright. But Whiteside was always dragging his feet, looking over his shoulder, worrying that the devil would grab his coattails.

As three heavily armed riders led the galloping legion up the street, Murdock saw greasy, grimy faces, lank, long hair, dead merciless eyes, and drawn guns everywhere.

Quickly backing inside, he slammed the door and

yelled at his teller, "Lock up! Lock the money in the safe!"

The massed riders came on with irresistible force as Doc Wallace opened his office door. He stared for a moment at the onrushing cavalcade, then saw Ellen playing in the middle of the street.

Leaping from the boardwalk with both hands outstretched, he caught the little girl, dragged her back to the boardwalk and on into the examining room of his office.

"Let me go!" the little yellow-haired girl cried out, struggling against the gray-haired doctor's hands, which held her like claws.

"Hush, child!" The doctor tried to calm her. "There's too many of them."

As the riders gathered in front of the jail, the doctor whispered, "Ellen, I want you to stay here while I go look. Will you do that?"

Almost directly across the street, one of the riders yelled, "Come on out, Marshal, and bring Herod with you!"

"Not a chance!" Marshal McKenzie yelled from inside the jail. "Get out of my town right now or I'll shoot him first."

"You want us to burn down every damn shack in this town, we'll do it!" another rider yelled back. "Just bring out Herod and we'll be gone."

Far outnumbered by the throng of riders, their six-guns drawn, their intent plain, Marshal McKenzie stood by the front door hoping the townspeople would commence firing from their buildings. The gang would have to split up, and most of them would run, and he'd at least have a fighting chance.

He thought of his daughter and wished he knew where she was.

He knew he couldn't kill Herod in cold blood, if only because he'd lose his only leverage.

"Let's blow hell out of him, Sinjun!" an outlaw bellowed.

The marshal poked his Colt out the doorway without showing himself, and yelled, "You men leave town right now!"

In less than a second a volley of slugs slammed into the open doorway, with at least three of them hitting his gun, one clipping off his second finger, and another breaking through his knuckles.

Retreating, McKenzie reached for the shotgun hanging on the wall with his left hand, but as he tried to load it with one hand, the door filled with onrushing gunmen.

"Get the keys!" Herod commanded from his cell. "And don't kill him yet."

One of the leaders grabbed the iron key ring from the wall and unlocked the cell.

"Did you remember to bring a cigar along?" Herod asked quietly.

"Yes, sir. I got half a dozen." A man with a cast in one eye and a missing front tooth proudly handed over a pack of long cheroots wrapped in a greasy bandanna.

"Jesus!" Herod said with disgust, putting the

cigars in his inner coat pocket, tossing the filthy neckerchief aside.

The marshal, his hands shackled behind his back, felt the burning pain shoot up his right arm and wanted to vomit, but he forced himself to stand erect and swallow the bitter bile. He was defeated, his gun hand maimed, but he wasn't whipped.

"What do you want?" he asked Herod.

"I've already taken it." His voice was soft and bland as Mississippi mud.

"You can't stay," Marshal McKenzie said. "You can burn and rob the town, I guess, but you can't stay."

"You see, that's where you made your mistake, Marshal," Herod said contemptuously. "I was thinking this was just a pokey little town until you put me in that cell."

"You've forgot the Federal marshals," McKenzie said.

"The nearest Federal marshal is off way to hell and gone, and he's not going to worry himself about Redemption, especially if he knows he's going to get killed if he sticks his nose into my town's business."

"There's a lot of good people live in this town, Herod," McKenzie said, trying to believe it.

"Hardworking, productive, prosperous folks," Herod chuckled, "and about as gutless as a dairy full of milk cows. Don't worry, I won't hurt them. All they have to do is what they've always done. Make money. Of course, we'll split it, but as the wise man said, 'Half a loaf is better than none.'"

"Take my advice," the young marshal said, "ride for Mexico. Maybe you can take over a village down there and nobody will mind, but you can't do it here."

"You're not listening, Marshal. I've already taken it." Herod's voice lost its soft, unguent quality and turned hard as iron. "This is *my* town now. I own it. I'll kill anybody that thinks otherwise, and I'm going to start with you."

"You don't have to," McKenzie said, looking at the floor. "My hand is ruined. I'm no threat to anybody anymore. I'd just like to take my little girl and ride out."

"You finally figured your townsfolk aren't goin' to come to your rescue?" Herod chuckled dryly.

"Likely they'll suffer for it, too," McKenzie said, downcast.

"Any problems out there, Freels?" Herod asked a broad-shouldered, potbellied ape of a man.

"Quiet as a tree full of possums." Freels grinned. "I tried runnin' down a girl out in the street when we rode in, but she got away from me."

"You sonofabitch!" McKenzie yelled, lunging forward, kicking Freels in the belly.

Freels rocked backward, gasping for breath, and Herod said to Sinjun, "Give him a little lick."

Sinjun immediately swung his gun barrel against McKenzie's head with enough force to drive him to one knee, his torso wobbling back and forth as he tried to absorb the blow.

"You tamed down yet, Marshal?" Herod asked softly.

"Just let my daughter and me loose," McKenzie stammered, staring at the floor. "I'll never say a word about you or this town to anybody."

"You sound like you're whipped, Marshal," Herod murmured. "You think you're whipped?"

"Yes, sir, I reckon I'm as whipped as a man can be."

"I didn't hear you, Marshal," Herod murmured, a mean glint in his eye.

"I said I'm whipped and I'm begging you for my life and my little girl's," the marshal said loudly, looking up, meeting Herod's eyes.

"You're askin' for my pity," Herod said, wanting the marshal to grovel before him.

"Pity, mercy, charity . . ."

"Yet you sneaked into my room and stuck a shotgun in my face when I was sleeping. You weren't thinking about pity and mercy then, were you?"

"No, sir, I was not. I was just doing my duty."

Perhaps nothing could save his daughter, although McKenzie prayed one of the townspeople would be good enough to send her back to her mother's family in Chicago. There was nowhere else.

He regarded himself as a dying man trying to set right his responsibilities, but he had no one to ask for help. Mr. Whiteside, Mr. Murdock, Doc Wallace . . . where were they when they were needed most? Off cowering in their root cellars, likely.

Sizing it up, McKenzie accepted his death, and once realizing his begging would achieve nothing, he stood straighter and waited.

"What's the matter, Marshal?" Herod asked. "Cat got your tongue?"

"You will die by the gun, Herod," McKenzie said simply.

"And I won't whine either. I won't beg for help. I won't grovel for mercy," Herod said sharply.

"It was because I was worrying about my daughter. Now I'm not worrying about anything."

"You just think so, Marshal." Herod chuckled, his eyes gleaming with anticipation. "You don't ever want to underestimate the quality of a southerner's sense of revenge. I mean, Marshal, we want it all. We want every crumb of the loaf, every scrap of the money. We want everything—including the toenails, and most of all, we want our mindless and unreconciled spirit to be known for what it is."

"You're as crazy as a damn bedbug," McKenzie said, no longer afraid.

"Crazy like a fox, maybe," Herod said, shrugging, "because I've won my town and I'm going to see you hang."

"I'm ready," McKenzie said.

"I'm not," Herod said bleakly. "I want your little girl to watch your face turn blue and your tongue stick out while you pee your pants. And you was sayin' how you was goin' to take me over to Tucson and they'd hang me two or three times, ain't that right?" Herod asked, his voice deep, resonant, redolent with good humor.

"Yes, sir, Mr. Herod." McKenzie nodded. "That's what I said."

"Well, then, it seems only fair to me as the new mayor of this town that I ought to hang you two or three times. Wouldn't you agree, Marshal?"

"I'm at your mercy," McKenzie said, "but I'd be beholden to you, sir, if you'd just let my little girl and me go on our way."

"Sinjun, go find his kid," Herod said sharply. "Little girls grow up to be big girls, and you never know, sometimes they turn out to be real nice."

"You wouldn't—" McKenzie's voice faltered.

"Marshal, the late war deprived me of what was rightfully mine. The mansion, the plantation and the darkies that worked it. It also did nothing to help the fortunes of my friends here," Herod said languidly. "Against our will, we must take by force what we want. We are not to blame. Your world is to blame."

McKenzie realized then there was no limit to Herod's brutality, because he blamed his vengeance and hatred on something else. It didn't make any difference if you owned a plantation or were a sharecropper with one mule, if the plantation or the mule was gone, then there was no way up but by your bootstraps. If you hadn't the bootstraps or the guts to start all over again, then you would become one of these.

There was no hope of mercy. His death was imminent. Herod was simply satisfying his lust for revenge by letting him hope there was some charity in his heart.

McKenzie saw clearly that nothing could change Herod. Nothing could change his men. Nothing could save his own life.

"Too bad, Herod," McKenzie said, "you might have amounted to something."

"I am more than something! I rule!" Herod yelled, his mask of affability lost.

"Maybe," McKenzie said. "Maybe not."

"Freels, didn't I see a ridgepole sticking out of the roof of this building? Didn't I see the Union flag hanging from that ridge pole?" Herod snapped out.

"Yes, sir, there's a ridgepole. They's a flag, too."

"Then let's hang this milksoppy marshal from the same pole his flag flaps on," Herod said, calming down. "Get a chair and a rope. Take this dutiful sonofabitch outside."

Alone and uncertain, little Ellen crept out of the examining room and saw Doc Wallace peering out of the slightly opened front door.

Ellen moved quietly to stand next to the doctor, where she peeked through the crack between door and jamb, and saw her father being brought outside. She watched the faces of the men around him. The half-breed, the hollow-cheeked one with the missing front tooth, the blond ape, but most of all the tall, broad-shouldered gentleman in the gray frock coat, carelessly smoking a long cheroot and giving orders so softly she couldn't hear; but she could see how the others obeyed instantly.

She had been raised on the mythology of King Arthur and the Knights of the Round Table and a gentle Jesus who loved all children. She was in no way prepared for the horror of the Monster. At first she thought it was only a bad dream that had come with the thunder, that in a moment her daddy's hand would touch her forehead and she would hear him say, "It's all right, Ellen. It's all right."

She heard nothing except Doc Wallace growling, "They wouldn't . . ."

Ellen watched the men stand her father on an oak chair with a spindle back. She saw the rope flung over the ridgepole just behind the flag, then the noose drawn tightly about her father's neck.

He was not praying, he was looking away at the mountains.

The rope tightened and his face remained impassive, his eyes fixed off in the distance.

"Get away from that chair," the Monster ordered, and as the lesser monsters moved away, his right hand suddenly leaped like a snake and came up with a six-gun. Within that blur, his finger touched the trigger, and in the bloom of fire and smoke, one leg of the chair was blown to splinters.

"One at a time, Marshal," Herod said. "You want to count?"

"It's nothing to me now."

BLAM! The second 280-grain bullet took out

another leg of the chair, which now teetered under the marshal's boots.

"Damn it!" Doc Wallace muttered under his breath. "Why doesn't somebody do something!"

BLAM! The third leg went, the chair moved wildly back and forth, ready to collapse.

"No!" she cried out.

Her small voice pierced the silence of the street, and Herod strolled over to the doctor's office and pushed the door open wide. "Look who's hiding in here." He smiled.

The doctor was fleeing out the back door, and only the small child waited for the nightmare to end.

Leading the little girl into the street, Herod said, "Come along, dear child. I'm going to give you a chance to save your daddy."

In front of the marshal's office, Herod put his arm around her shoulders and looked into her eyes. "There's your poor daddy. He's goin' to be hung unless somebody helps him out. Understand, little girl?"

Ellen had no reply. Frozen in terror and confusion, she only wanted the nightmare to end.

"Now listen to me, honey-punkin' child—I'm goin' to give you a chance to set your daddy free." Herod's voice was soft as molasses. "All you got to do is shoot that rope—and I'll turn him loose. Can you do that?"

She couldn't comprehend the words the man was saying. It had to be a dream.

"Yes, sir," she said weakly.

Putting the huge .44 Colt in her two hands, Herod smiled. "Now, aim at the rope and pull the trigger."

The weapon, weighing more than three pounds, was hard for her to hold up. She knew how to aim, with the front sight settled in the bottom of the notch of the back sight, because her daddy had explained it once, but she couldn't hold the heavy gun steady.

BLAM! The revolver roared and kicked back in her hands. The bullet was a yard too high, and her father said quietly, "Sweetheart, aim real close. You might just hit it and these folks just might do what they said."

"I can't!" she cried out helplessly.

"Aim real careful, Ellen," her father said patiently. "Remember how I showed you?"

She wanted to say "I'm trying," but the terror in her heart held her back.

"One more time," Herod said, smiling.

She closed her left eye and tried to aim, but the heavy pistol wobbled in her hands and she desperately squeezed the trigger. The bullet tore into the flag moving idly in the breeze above her daddy's head.

"You only have one more bullet, little girl," Herod said. "Make it count."

"Ellen, listen," her father said, trying to give her one last reassurance. "Don't worry, none of this is your fault. Don't blame yourself! I love you. I'll always love you, no matter what. Now—try again. Aim real close! Real close!"

The chair creaked and wobbled on its single leg,

ready to collapse. "Just squeeze the trigger real slow. . . ."

She tried to hold the gun steady and to squeeze at the same time.

The six-gun roared. A bluish red hole appeared in her father's forehead before his whole powerful body slumped like a rag doll and he hung there. She stared at the gun in her hands, and remembering the ominous thunder, she felt it drumming the dark horror in her brain and she screamed, "Daddy! Oh, Daddy!"

And the thunder rolled on and on. . . .

— 1 —

Gʀᴇᴀᴛ Bᴀsɪɴ ᴄᴏᴜɴᴛʀʏ. Rᴏᴄᴋ-ᴄᴜʀsᴇᴅ ᴡɪᴛʜ ɢʀᴀɴɪᴛᴇ ridges and snowy peaks, scored with long valleys that collected the sparse moisture and sometimes ran streams to join farther south and form a river. Grama and mesquite grass grew in the valleys as well as broad swatches of sagebrush, and higher on the sides of the ridges, junipers, piñons, cedars, and oaks thrived according to their elevation.

It was a land of lizard eaters, where even ranches were scarce and towns scarcer, depending upon the water.

Yet, despite the emptiness, travelers stopped to dig with pick and shovel, on the theory that if the convoluted land was so hostile, then surely it must be laden with precious metals.

Dog Kelly was a different breed of prospector. He knew the gold was close by because there was the notch in the mountain, there was the white rock so big it would take exactly seven Indians holding hands to circle it, and here was the lightning-blasted pine tree. You make the lineup; you walk due east fifteen paces and dig.

It said so on his map, and the map didn't lie because he'd drawn it himself.

Yet something was wrong. He'd dug five fruitless holes so far and was well into the sixth, and it wasn't easy digging. Kelly had been at it a week, and his mule was gaunt from foraging on sagebrush. His camp consisted only of a makeshift brush arbor, his bedroll, an iron pot half full of ham hocks and beans hanging over the fire, and the treasure map laid out on the sand and weighted down with rocks at each corner.

The notched mountain, the white boulder, the blasted pine tree. Fifteen paces east.

Maybe he should have wrote down west instead of east, he thought. Maybe it was north, maybe south. He couldn't remember now. Still, it had to be close by. If somebody'd dug it up, they'da left a hole, and there'd been no holes here when he'd come back.

Of medium height, his face was burned to the same color as his filthy butternut pants and shirt. He believed bathing opened the skin up to disease and pestilence. His greasy hair hung down to his shoulders and was tied back with a rattlesnake skin. His eyes were red-rimmed from the sun's glare and from the sharp-edged dust of the desert, and sometimes they seemed to turn over backward, staring back into his aching head.

Shunned by people, he had only his mule to talk to, and he hated the mule for being uppity.

"You black-assed son of a whore, which is it—east or west?" Dog Kelly demanded, climbing out of the empty hole.

The mule pointed one ear east, the other west, and drowsed in the shade of the brush arbor.

Kelly glared at the animal fiercely, his eyes deranged and painful. Thinking his eyes were about to roll over and peer inside his brain again, he covered them with his forearm and took a deep breath, telling himself that it couldn't be done. Eyes couldn't roll over.

As he tried to talk some sense to himself, he heard an iron-shod hoof ring on a rock in the distance and instantly dropped his arm and looked off across the rock-jumbled, glaring land. Shielding his eyes with his hand, he picked out a lone rider coming his way.

Cursing, he grabbed up his treasure map, folded it quickly and stuffed it into his bedroll. Seizing his old Sharps .50, he laid the barrel on a head-high sandstone boulder and waited until the rider closed the distance enough for a fair shot.

Sighting down the rusty barrel, his mouth stretched sidewise in a derisive grin, Kelly squeezed the soft trigger. The blast made his ears ring and the recoil knocked him backward, but, recovering quickly, he saw the rider pitch from the saddle and lie still.

Warily, Kelly approached the crumpled form dressed in golden buckskin pants and tunic, lying facedown. Holding the Sharps ready, he circled the body, but there was no movement. Coming close, he prodded at it with the muzzle of the rifle.

Nothing.

Roughly, he rolled the body over and stepped back in surprise and wonder. It looked like a woman. A goddamn good looker, too. All that yellow hair, creamy skin—and a blouse full of bosom, too.

Bending over, he felt her breasts and forgot to wonder why there wasn't any blood.

Nice, soft tits. He smiled and laid the rifle aside. As he bent over to pull up the shirt, the woman suddenly brought her right hand around with a Colt .44 locked in it, smacking him on the side of the jaw.

Falling away from the force of the blow, he landed in a pile of rocks, and as he groaned and tried to get to his feet, he saw her standing above him, a powerful, long-waisted woman. Her leather slouch hat had a bullet hole through it, and he silently cussed his fool eyes for making him miss what should have been an easy shot.

Quickly, he rolled and reached for the rifle, and without a word of warning or fear, she slammed her left boot down on his hand and, drawing back her right leg, kicked him just below the ear.

His mad, inflamed eyes rolled up, his head lolled, and his body went slack.

Hardly pausing, she dragged him to the base of the blasted pine, and taking a set of manacles from her saddlebag, she passed them through a rotted-out hole in the stump and locked them tightly on his wrists.

Taking her time, she searched the camp, and after looking at the treasure map, tossed it aside. In his shirt pocket she found a folded-up flyer:

REDEMPTION
QUICK DRAW JAMBOREE

Open to anyone brave enough
to shoot with anybody else
First Prize $$124,000.$$
July 1–4

Lighting a slim black cigarillo, she folded the flyer, slipped it into her pocket, and studied the unconscious form of Dog Kelly.

Picking up his canteen, she pulled the stopper and poured water down on his filthy face.

Dog sputtered and yelped from the shock, opened his roving mad eyes and glared up at her. "You bitch of a whore devil!" he cursed, and lunged at her, only to find he was locked to the stump.

"This the trail to Redemption?" she asked, eyeing him closely.

"No," he snarled. "It goes over to Yuma."

She nodded. "I figured you'd lie."

"Don't leave me out here in the sun!" he yelled as she started to turn away. "That'd be like murder!"

"I suppose." She nodded agreeably.

"Wait!" he screamed. "What'd I ever do to you?"

"You ruined my forty-dollar hat," she said, and not looking back, mounted her black gelding and rode southwest down the trail.

"Bitch-dog! Rotten nauch! You two-bit piece of ass!" he screamed. "You stump-suckin' sonofabitch! You Indian fucker! I'm goin' to ram a stick of dynamite up your slot and light it off! By God, I'm goin' to strip you naked and spur you to death, I am!"

But she was long gone, and as the sun scalded his unprotected face, he arched his back, braced his knees, and pulled as hard as he could against the old stump.

Toward dusk she came to the ford. The river was nearly dry, and its scattered pools were covered with green slime and stank of rotting fish.

On the far bank stood an old sign so peppered with bullet holes she could hardly make out the lettering: REDEMPTION.

Next to the sign a man hung dead from an old bullet-scarred tree.

Crossing over, she paused to study the rising ground and the town beyond. Snaking down the hillside was an oversized graveyard, the markers poking out of the ground like dozens of chipped teeth. Gaunt mongrel dogs prowled through the graveyard and ravens roosted in the bare limbs of dead trees.

A shudder passed through her body, an instinctive and fearful revulsion that told her to go the other way, go anywhere but not ahead through the gates of hell.

Still she kneed the black horse up the rise, not because she wanted to, but because she had to.

It was almost twilight as she rode down the main street mounded with windrows of horse manure at the hitch rails. She passed by a dead hound dog with barbed wire wrapped around its neck. A group of youngsters were teasing a fat, drunken squaw squatting on the splintered boardwalk. She saw a number of men dressed in lurid western costumes that seemed to cry out, "Look at me! Look at me!" Those men had eyes of flint and wore their six-guns tied low on their thighs.

She passed a cowboy on his hands and knees vomiting in the street.

The twenty-some buildings, sandblasted by the wind, huddled against each other with cracked windows and swaybacked roof lines. She passed by the marshal's office and jail, which had been blasted and burned and left as a warning.

Her full lips tightened with a flicker of fear despite her hard-won discipline.

Those townspeople on the boardwalk who had the temerity to look at her did so quickly and averted their eyes to study the horse manure or count the holes in the boardwalk.

She realized that the town made nothing and served no one except the gunmen leaning against the walls or staggering zigzag fashion across the street.

The old church at the end of the street had been added onto with a brick wing on either side. In the belfry a man with a carbine stood silhouetted against the dying sun.

Outside his carpentry shop, a middle-aged black man was planing a wide, flat board, and as she passed by, he looked up, eyed her a moment, and murmured, "Five-foot-eight. Am I right?"

She didn't answer, but she saw that the board was meant to be a coffin lid.

She saw the bullet-shattered sign STOCKMAN'S REST hanging over the broad veranda, and out of the corner of her eye she saw on the balcony four hard-eyed, bored women in garish dresses adorned with feathers, glass beads, and German silver chains, shaving and manicuring a man who was staring down at her.

His brutal, pockmarked face looked like a moldy cheese, and she thought you could hit him with a whiskey jug and he wouldn't blink. Despite his loutish features, he was dressed in gray flannel trousers, an open-throated red silk shirt, and a bright blue sateen frock coat.

Obviously the prince of whores, he studied her long form as she rode by and muttered to his sporters loud enough for her to hear, "She don't put out, but she'd like to."

The sporters cackled obligingly, and she felt the tension rising in the town as the sun settled in the west and darkness signaled danger.

Approaching the middle of town, she saw the clock

tower and heard the minute hand jerk with a rasping crunch and the grinding of gears as the chime struck seven times.

Halting the black, she saw that the two-story bank on the corner had been converted into a saloon with a shoeshine stand near the front door where a boy was shining the boots of an elegantly dressed Mexican.

Reining the black to the hitch rail, she dismounted beside a handsome gray thoroughbred branded on the hip with an ace of spades. Its black saddle was tooled and carved with graceful flourishes and adorned with polished silver conchas.

The Mexican stood, dug a nail from his vest pocket and dropped it into the shoeshine boy's tin cup.

She looked at the boy and saw that he was blind. Next to the shoeshine stand was an old trunk with fold-out trays divided into small compartments holding a great variety of small things. Cigars, matches, handkerchiefs, gold-plated stickpins. Pencils and erasers, pens and inks, collar buttons and cartridges, playing cards and dice, fingernail files and jackknives.

"Evening, ma'am," the boy said. "Welcome to the Old Bank Saloon."

She passed her hand in front of his eyes and he didn't blink.

"You're a little young to be working the street, aren't you?" she asked.

"I'm on my own. I like it that way."

"You know you took a nail in your cup instead of a dime?"

The boy nodded. "I know. That was Carlos Montoya. He thinks he's a big-time outlaw, but he's just a runt, and every time he cheats me, I know his cheating will help finish him off."

"How old are you? Ten?" she asked harshly.

"That's close enough. Don't worry, I know what I'm doing."

"I'm not worrying," she said curtly, and walked across the veranda of the old bank and pushed through the bat-wing doors.

The turned walnut spindles that had once separated the customers from the teller had been removed, leaving the counter as a bar. She wondered why there were so few people and then remembered it was the quiet hour between the afternoon and the night. Off to her left she saw a half-dozen white leather bags bearing the black ace of spades emblem piled by a table next to a pair of white leather boots. From the boots she looked up to the man sitting at the card table.

Dressed in black calfskin trousers and jacket, with a black silk shirt and white silk neckerchief, he was at once handsome and venomous. In an elaborately tooled black leather gun belt were holstered two pearl-handled silver inlaid Colt Peacemakers, and in his hands was a deck of cards being shuffled by his long, dexterous fingers.

"Ace Hanlon, ma'am. Care for a friendly game of poker?"

"You look like you're doing all right playing with yourself," she said.

"This is a special deck." A little smiled played over his thin lips. "I put an ace in every time I kill a man."

In a blur he flipped the deck to the green felt and fanned open the cards. All aces.

"I like one-eyed jacks," she said, turning away and moving to the end of the bar where the string bean of a barman stood on a stool, putting a full bottle on the top shelf.

"Whores next door," he said without looking down.

"You—" she said.

"I said whores next door," the bartender repeated loudly.

Suddenly, she kicked the bottom rung of the stool, sending it skittering away, leaving the lanky bartender in midair with the bottle in his hand.

Falling, he lost the bottle and cracked his nose on the back bar, his head whipping back as he yelped "Oh hell," and cried out in pain.

She caught the flying bottle, set it in front of her on the bar and said, "A bath and a room, if it's not too much trouble."

Ace Hanlon chuckled and, putting down the cards, clapped his hands together softly and said, "Bravo, lady."

"Bath and a room coming up," the bartender whimpered from the duckboards and slowly got to his feet.

Jerking the cork from the bottle with her teeth, she said, "I'll have a Dead-Eye while I'm waiting."

"Yes'm," the bartender said quickly. "Right away . . ." Frowning, he asked in confusion, "Pardon me, ma'am, don't get mad now, but what exactly is a Dead-Eye?"

Upending the bottle into a beer mug, she poured it half full. "Six shots of rye," she said, grinning maliciously, "with a dead eyeball in it."

As she reached over the bar, the bartender flinched, but she only wanted the bowl of black olives, and picking out a plump one, plunked it into the whiskey.

"Now you know," she said, and took a healthy drink. "Maybe you better write it down."

"I guess I can recall that, ma'am," the bartender stammered. "Six shots of rye and one black olive."

"Sometimes you can change it and put in a cherry instead of the olive."

"What do they call that, ma'am?" the bartender asked, wide-eyed.

"A Chicago virgin."

"Yes'm . . ." The bartender blushed and strangled out, "The thing is, there ain't no cherries in this town."

"One-eyed jacks are wild," Ace Hanlon said to her back.

"That's why I like 'em," she said, and carrying her drink, she walked out to the veranda and took a seat on the shoeshine stand.

Staring out into the dusk, she felt that it was a

town of the night, when violent death and rankest corruption could be observed as simply a normal way of life. The town's people would be at home all snug and tidy, flinching at every report of a six-gun, trembling at every distant dying scream, and dreading to open the door in the morning to see what horror awaited them.

The blind boy commenced cleaning her short boots as she sipped at her drink and tried to feel the dimensions of human decay in this town called Redemption.

"Interested in French brandy, ma'am? I've also got some Egyptian cigarettes, India ink, black, green, or red—"

"Just shine the boots," she said, and looked up the street at the church. The cross was gone from the top of the belfry, but the life-sized marble statue of Jesus as a pastor, both hands extended as if to welcome little children, still stood in the yard, centered between the two wings made of burned brick.

"John Herod owns that big house," the blind boy said. "He's mayor."

She stared at the boy as he bent over her boots. How could he know what she was looking at or what she was thinking?

"He gets fifty cents of every dollar in this town," the boy said.

"What's the town get in return?" she asked indifferently.

"It gets to stay alive." The boy grinned.

She saw three men wearing tan-colored dusters

and carrying rifles step out onto the broad front porch, and a brass-bound telescope poke out of the window above them.

The glass swept the street and paused a long moment as it aimed at her, then passing on, it moved to observe the far end of the street.

"Another gun comin' to town," the blind boy said.

She heard hoofbeats and saw a rider coming at a full gallop down the main street.

A few yards from the saloon, the rider sat back in the saddle and jerked the reins, forcing the horse to sit back and slide on its raw hocks to a stop at the hitch rail.

Stepping down from the horse, the big rider, hulking like he was carrying a heavy weight on his shoulders, headed for the saloon.

Only when he came closer in the dim light did she see that the rider was a human tattoo, a shocking testament to self-mutilation. His body art was prison art, hideout art, waiting time art, done with knife blades, pins, awls, nails sharpened on jailhouse floors in order to incise the black soot into his skin. With his shirtsleeves torn off at the shoulders, she could see the skull and crossbones, the names, a motto NO BARS FOR SCARS, a fouled anchor, a six-gun shooting a bullet into the arm, a buzzard or an eagle, a snake slithering out of his armpit. Across his broad, flat face was a jagged scar in the shape of an X, and on his left arm was a ladder of twenty pearly welts, like notches on a tree trunk.

"That's Scars," the boy said sotto voce as the big hulking man stomped up the steps into the saloon.

"What does he do besides carve up his hide?"

"Kills." The boy shrugged. "Just like the rest of them." Then by way of explanation, he murmured, "You see, they know they're safe here."

"Because of John Herod?"

"He's boss." The boy nodded as the bat-wing doors slammed open and a man flew out head first, cartwheeling down the steps to the street. Nearly weeping, the man moaned, "No, no, no," and leaped onto his mustang in terror. Gigging his spurs and slapping the reins, he raced up the street.

In a moment, Scars strolled out the door, a schooner of beer in his left hand and a six-gun in the other. Blowing the foam off his beer, he took a deep draught, belched, and watched the rider galloping out of town.

"Gettin' dark," he complained, lifted the six-gun, and aiming with his head cocked sidewise, his right eye squinting, he squeezed the trigger.

As if he'd been hit in the back by a sledgehammer, the man arched his shoulders backward and lost his reins. Slipping sideways, he lost his right stirrup and slid off the near side of the panicked mustang. The rider's left boot hung in the stirrup as he fell. The bouncing of his head and shoulders on the ground terrified the pony all the more, until they were lost in the darkness.

"Sonofabitch," Scars said, holstering the six-gun.

Taking the foot-long Bowie from its scabbard, he extended his left arm and made a quick slash.

Blood oozed from the cut and Scars carefully restored the knife to the sheath, reached into his shirt pocket for a packet of white crystalline powder, poured it on the wound and smiled.

"That's just plain salt," he said. "It sets a good solid scar."

His tittering giggle changed to hilarious laughter which moved on to a powerful guffaw as he looked admiringly at his arm.

"That makes twenty-one!" he burst out proudly.

"Why?" she asked.

"He was a blabbermouth and I just got out," Scars said, as if he were explaining two plus two.

"Congratulations," she said, her irony lost on him.

"They put me up for a hundred and ninety years, but then I was a good boy and they let me out early." Scars's voice was weakly childish.

"How long did you do this time?" the blind boy asked.

"Maybe a week," the hulking man said. "I lose track of time, y'know."

"Then I guess it doesn't make any difference," she said.

"You here for the Jamboree?" Scars asked, his strange, befuddled eyes staring at her.

"That's right."

"Will they let you in?"

"They damn well better," she said shortly.

"They won't," he said, frowning. "Nobody would shoot with a pretty lady like you."

"It's not a question of man or woman. The Colt is the equalizer," she replied, half smiling.

"I'm pretty fast," Scars said.

"And you shoot pretty straight, I guess. Were you trying for a head shot?"

"I'd be a liar if I said I was," Scars said slowly. "I shot for his backbone figuring if I went high, I'd take off his head."

"You're smarter'n you look," she said. "What else do you do besides shoot people in the back?"

"I shoot 'em in the front or sidewise. It don't make a never-mind to me," Scars said, eyeing her hungrily, and added, "I ain't had a woman for a day and a half."

"Jesus," she said, shaking her head.

"You're purty enough."

"Whores are next door."

"I'll show you a good time," he said, smiling broadly.

She shook her head. "I'll loan you fifty cents and you can show somebody else a good time."

"I got plenty of money. I'll buy you diamonds big as horse turds," Scars said earnestly, bending down, talking seriously. "I mean, you're just as pretty a piece of poontang I ever saw."

"You need a bath, Scars, and you need to gargle some boiled sagebrush."

"That ain't very friendly talk," the big man said,

frowning. "Supposin' I just ripped off your clothes right here and give you a good poke."

"Maybe you better ask Mr. Herod first," the blind boy said.

For a moment Scars froze as he interpreted the simple statement, then knowing he was beaten, gritted out, "Aw hell, I wouldn't let my dog go at you."

The blind boy understood the tone of voice and moved quickly aside, knowing exactly what was going to happen because he had opened his big mouth.

Scars looked at her, looked at the boy, then booted the trunk full of miscellany off the porch into the street.

Standing back, he laughed loudly and said in his high-pitched child's voice, "Oh my! I'm so clumsy!" Still laughing, he added, "I must be blind!"

Carrying her saddlebags over her left shoulder, she climbed the stairway to the second floor of the saloon. The carpet on the steps was threadbare and smelled of cat urine. On the dingy walls were pinned wanted posters, autographed as if it were an honor to have your picture shown in that gallery. Among the faces, she picked out Scars's instantly, and read that he was worth a thousand dollars dead or alive and was wanted for murder, rape, assault to commit murder, and robbery.

For a moment she stared at a hollow-cheeked stranger with deranged eyes, trying to remember where she'd seen him. Wanted for murder and bank robbery, his bounty was only five hundred dollars. When she read the name Leonard Kelly, she remembered the bushwhacker in the desert, and went on up the stairs to the narrow corridor.

Looking through more wanted posters, she searched for a face that was not there, and proceeded on down the corridor with a worried frown creasing her forehead.

One of the doors was partly open as she passed by, and she heard hushed voices murmuring their discontent. Glancing inside, she saw nine or ten townspeople gathered around a table whispering cautiously.

She couldn't hear what they were saying, but she could see them emptying out cigar boxes and leather poke bags onto the table in front of a well-dressed black man with a shaved head. His wide-set eyes watched the pile of money on the table grow. Lean, wiry, in his early forties, he seemed to emanate the same portent of death as Ace Hanlon downstairs, the coldly confident air of the professional assassin.

A journeyman, she thought, a master of his trade.

The wide-set eyes flicked up to the door, saw her face, and his straight-across mouth moved. In a moment a man with his back to her turned and quietly closed the door.

Continuing on down the hallway, she came to an open door where a dark-haired girl, hardly fourteen years old, was arranging blankets on a cot. The room was small, squalid, and smelled of rat droppings, but the girl had swept the floor clean and piled boxes and sacks out in the corridor.

"Afternoon, ma'am." The girl turned to face her. "My name's Katie. The barman downstairs, he's my dumb daddy, and you're . . . ?"

"Here," she said.

"This'll have to do 'cause there ain't nowhere else during kill week," Katie chattered on, intrigued by the straight-backed, handsome lady. "You from back East?"

She stepped forward, and taking Katie's wrist, led her to the doorway.

"Don't mind my daddy, he's just old-fashioned. You look like you've been riding a long time. I don't get a chance to talk to normal people much. . . . You here for the jamboree? The bath's down at the end of the hall. I fired up the boiler for you. . . ."

At the doorway, realizing she was being a nuisance, she said simply, "I guess I better go now."

The lady nodded and closed the door.

=== 2 ===

BLAM BLAM BLAM BLAM BLAM BLAM!

Six shots rang out and she dived off the cot to the floor, six-gun in hand.

Then she woke up. There was no one else in the room; the shooting came from down in the street.

"Damn fool," she chided herself sheepishly, "the hot bath made you sleepy."

Sitting on the cot had felt so good, she'd lain her head down for just a moment, tired and drowsy, and drifted off into a deep sleep.

Lifting the window shade, she saw that the street had been transformed into a strange carnival. Oil lanterns were strung up and down the street and people milled by canvas-sided booths, or gambled on brightly painted wheels of fortune. Banners announcing the Quick Draw Jamboree were strung up over the street.

Get your guts up, lady, she told herself, paste on a cardboard face and be smart.

Setting her slouch hat at a cocky angle, she went downstairs and, mingling with the crowd, saw how people were divided into townsmen staying in their shops, peering worriedly outside, and crazed ruffians staggering down the boardwalk, some dragging a bangled, flouncy whore along, in effect, occupying the town. There seemed to be no organization, no control, and no law.

She paused to watch a couple of bare-chested men cracking long bullwhips in a carney stall, breaking whiskey bottles that a dwarf set up for them. The poppers sounded like pistol shots as they cracked near the stumpy-legged dwarf and the men roared with laughter.

In another booth, men threw knives at a picture of a nude woman bending over. Vendors passed through the crowd selling cigars, chewing tobacco and snuff, bright neckerchiefs, silk hat bands, Mexican twenty-point spurs, cotton blankets, and patent medicines.

As she walked slowly down the boardwalk, she passed three back-alley whores, toothless slatterns who'd played their time out.

"What ya packin', dearie?" one yelled.

"She walks like she's got a ramrod up her ass!" another hooted.

"Give us a bit of something for old times' sake."

Not answering, she walked on.

She paused to watch two drink-maddened men fighting each other with fence posts, and watched others laying and taking bets on which one would survive.

A young man, blind drunk, staggered past, endlessly calling out his sales pitch: "Gold teeth here! Getcher gold teeth here! All sizes, guaranteed to fit. Gold teeth. Gold teeth here!"

On up the street a one-legged man was cranking a hurdy-gurdy, his hat on the ground with a few pennies in it.

Listening to the hurdy-gurdy, she noticed an old man standing in a doorway staring at her. His hair was white and his skin nearly transparent. His old eyes had receded back into their sockets and looked like rusty nail heads. Over the door hung a faded sign: Walter D. Wallace, M.D.

The old man's face registered astonishment and fear, as if he'd just seen a messenger from hell.

She turned away and hurried up the street until she was impeded by a crowd of men gathered around a mechanical shooting game.

She watched the black mortician, Charles Moonlight, crank up the spring and move a lever that set loose a file of steel Indians attacking a painted wagon train. The Indians bobbed and weaved through enameled steel bushes. A man with a revolver fired six times, and Charles Moonlight called out, "Three out of six. Not bad shooting, but not good enough to win the cigar! Who's next? A quarter a play, step right up and save the wagons from the goddamned filthy bastardly Inju—"

The spiel broke off abruptly as Moonlight looked up at the six-foot-five-inch, burly-shouldered Indian wearing a black serge suit, but also wearing two eagle feathers in his braided hair.

Moonlight did an about-face and addressed the crowd on the other side, offering the reloaded pistol. "Only one-fourth of a dollar . . ."

"Mr. Dred, sir, good evening," Moonlight said, holding the pistol out to the man she had seen earlier on the veranda with his whores.

"Nice to see you, sir—"

She thought the ugly whoremonger looked all the more frightening because of his sartorial splendor.

"Shut up. Just shut your damn mouth," Dred said, ignoring the proffered Navy Colt and opening his tricolored satin frock coat to reveal a pair of gleaming nickel-plated revolvers.

With a pistol in each hand he watched the Indians bobbing out of the woods until he felt the rhythm of their appearance, then fired three shots from each pistol, his hands steady, his eyes true as six Indians went down.

"I'll take that cigar," the whoremonger named Eugene Dred rasped, and plucked the cigar from Moonlight's fingers.

Biting off the end of the cigar and spitting it to the ground, Dred struck a match and was about to light the cigar when a young man, hardly more than a youth, said with a taunting laugh, "Good enough shooting, Eugene. If I was a tin Injun, then I'd think about dusting out of town. . . ."

Dred looked at the good-looking, open-faced young man who stood cockily with his arm around a beaming young blond sporter wearing a low-cut dress covered with pink silk bows.

"But then, a metal Injun don't shoot back, does he?" the young man said cockily. "You better speed up your draw before somebody takes you for easy meat. And you're aiming left. You were lucky to nick that last Injun."

Eugene Dred said nothing, but drew the flame into the cigar, and when he was satisfied that it was smoking well, he glanced contemptuously at the young man and said, "You owe me money, Kid. You been pokin' my whore."

The Kid's face grew somber and he looked over at his petite, frozen-faced companion and said, "Mattie's my fiancée."

"Not while she's still my whore, she ain't," Eugene Dred rasped, then reaching past Charles Moonlight, he punched the lever that set the Indians to bobbing and weaving, and glaring at the Kid with cold-blooded murder in his eyes, added, "Step right up, Kid. Miss one single Indian and I'll kill you."

Cockily, the Kid grinned, looked Eugene Dred up and down, and said lightly, "Hell, that's too easy. Any old worn-out fart can hit 'em from here. I'll just step back a ways and make it interesting."

Stiff with rage, Eugene Dred watched the Kid move back five paces.

Opening his coat, the Kid revealed a matched pair of Smith & Wesson Schofield .45's, both silver inlaid, engraved, with carved ivory grips.

Turning around with his back to the Indians and facing the remodeled church, he looked up at the belfry and did a little frolicky dance step in a circle that brought him back to facing the shooting gallery. Carelessly, he made a little mock bow to Dred, then in a blur of energy quick-drew with his left hand and rapidly fired.

Five Indians collapsed almost as one and the sixth bullet tore the end of Dred's cigar off.

"Damn! I missed that last one!" The Kid laughed. "Guess I was pullin' to the left, too!"

The final Indian moved back and forth between bush and tree as the bystanders hushed and moved to clear a path between the two men. Silently, both men reloaded, and the nervous crowd edged farther back.

"A double eagle on the Kid," a bystander sang out.

"I'll take it," a man in a derby yelled back.

Loaded, the six-guns were slipped back into their holsters, and the two men faced each other.

Eugene Dred, flamboyant apeman, older, perhaps wiser, knew he would lose all if he let this brash youngster insult him.

And the Kid seemed to be just skylarking, blithely enjoying the killing game, fearlessly trying to make a fool out of the brute dressed like a dude dandy.

Grinning, the Kid knocked his knees together in

mock fear and chuckled, "Make your play, old-timer."

Dred's hand slowly moved toward his holster, and the Kid's hand kept pace until there was no more room to stop and talk it over.

In that frozen instant, BLAM, the Kid's hat was blown off. Dred stared at the Kid. He hadn't drawn yet, nor had the Kid. What the hell?

Dred turned along with the rest of the crowd to see where the bullet had come from when another BLAM followed and the rest of Dred's cigar disappeared from his clenched, swollen lips.

Before anyone could react, BLAM, down went the remaining Indian.

The crowd lunged to get free or dived to the ground in panic as BLAM BLAM, the two side struts of the shooting gallery fell.

The whole town was suddenly as silent as a dusty tomb.

She kept her feet in spite of the panic of the crowd and looked up the street at the converted church and saw that the double French doors were opened onto the veranda.

A gold-plated handgun appeared to be an extension of a silken dressing gown sleeve. Smoke curled slowly up from its muzzle as it held rock steady. Slowly the sleeve and revolver retreated back into the darkness, and after a moment the French doors closed.

The marble statue of the bearded Jesus extending

his hands stared back at the terrified crowd until the Kid laughed, strutted a circle around Mattie and yelled, "That's my pa! He's sayin' it's time to put up or shut up."

"Sign-up time!" somebody yelled, and the serious gunfighters separated themselves from the grifters and idle bystanders and moved toward the Old Bank Saloon.

She followed along. Feeling a hand clamp down on her butt, she dug an elbow back into the solar plexus of a solemn-faced cowboy, who suddenly jackknifed and gasped for air, with no one in the jam of people aware of what had happened.

In the crowded saloon she found a spare chair off to the side and tried to look invisible. Glancing off to the left, she saw that a whole range of outlaws were sitting beneath their own reward posters, most of them eyeing her with the look a hungry rattlesnake gives to a bunny rabbit.

The lanky bartender banged on the bar with a bung starter and yelled, "All right everybody, hold it down."

As the crowd quieted, he continued.

"My name's Horace Pinnick, and I'm declaring the Quick Draw Jamboree open. Are you ready to fight?"

Hoots and cheers erupted from the gunmen, and Horace grinned in welcome.

"Here's how it goes: Each man who enters will fight once a day. Anybody can challenge anybody and your fight time is pulled from a hat. For the duration of the Jamboree, all fighters will be served free anything they want, courtesy of Mr. Herod, and that means free grub, whiskey, and nauch. . . ."

"That ain't nothin'," Scars yelled back in his high-pitched voice. "Where's the money? What do we get paid?"

"Not a red cent," Horace replied steadily as the audience grumbled, "but the man who wins this contest takes the jackpot."

Pulling aside an old blanket, he revealed a brass-bound Wells Fargo money box. Lifting the lid of the box, he pulled out bundles of currency and held them high.

"There's a hundred and twenty-four thousand dollars in this box, courtesy of Wells Fargo and Mr. Herod," he announced.

All eyes fixed on the box hungrily, and she thought it didn't really make any difference. No one in the saloon would use it to buy a ranch or a business and go straight. No one would have the sense to put it into railroad bonds and live off the interest. Every damn one of them would throw it away as fast as possible on mindless whores, agile sharpers, or just give it away to hear somebody say thanks. In a matter of months the money'd all be pissed away, and it would be back to robbing the mail cars and banks again.

For a moment she felt like standing up and telling the whole damn bunch of them that they were just entertainers for John Herod, who wasn't in the business of paying out money, nor giving it away, neither.

Turning to a ruled blackboard on the back bar, Horace picked up a piece of chalk and asked loudly, "So, what do you say, gents? Have we got any real men here?"

A chair kicked back and a blue-eyed man with a full blond beard stood like a mountain and yelled in a strange brogue, "Put up Gutzon! I am champion shooter of Sweden!"

"Mr. Gutzon is the first to go up," Horace said, printing the name on the blackboard as the crowd roared its approval.

Ace Hanlon, all in black except for his white calfskin boots, stood up leisurely and surveyed the room like a disdainful king counting his lackeys.

"Ace Hanlon," he said clearly. "Draw a black ace and you'll know what that means."

Before the crowd could applaud, his hands stabbed to his Colts and, quick as a whiplash, his revolvers were twirling forward and backward with such speed no one was sure. Suddenly both pistols were in the air and had changed hands before anyone had time to absorb the first display. Once again they pinwheeled like bright stars in his hands, then abruptly the guns were back in their holsters and Ace Hanlon lifted both hands high and inclined his head to receive the deafening applause.

As Ace Hanlon returned to his chair, the Kid yelled across the room from his table, "Better put me and my friend Eugene on the list. Eugene, you know how to spell your name?"

Eugene Dred, from his table in the front row, glared over his shoulder at the Kid and angrily protested, "I didn't say nothin' about entering any damnfool contest—"

"I think I hear an old hen squawking." The Kid chuckled. "Has anybody sneaked a chicken in here?"

Dred rose and charged toward the Kid's table, but was met by half a dozen gunfighters who stood in his way like a wall.

"I can take you out with my bare hands! Right now!" Eugene Dred roared, his pockmarked face purple with rage.

"No, Eugeney," the Kid teased, lounging back in his chair, "it's a gunfight. Like we both have guns, right? We aim, we fire, you die . . . you'll figure it out as we go along."

Dred lunged against the men obstructing him, but to no avail, and after Horace had added the names to the list, he called out, "Please, gents, fighting begins tomorrow in the street and not in here. Who else is going up?"

"Sergeant Quanson," came the melodious voice of the black man with the shaven head.

She looked over and recognized him from the glimpse in the hall she'd had earlier. The calm, cold, efficient journeyman. The master of simple murder.

"How do you spell that?" Horace asked, trying to top-dog him.

"Correctly," Sergeant Quanson said succinctly.

Before there could be any more back and forth arrogance, the big Indian stepped up to the bar and plopped down a buckskin bag. Opening it, he laid out a horse carved from soapstone with a piece of turquoise nugget tied to its back, next was the transparent rattlesnake tail nearly three inches long and containing twenty-six rattles and a button, next came a quartz crystal like a six-sided gun barrel, and lastly came the joined upper and lower jawbones of a human with all its white teeth shining white and intact.

"Hold it there, Chief," Horace joked good-naturedly. "Set up your souvenir stand outside and send up a smoke signal."

The crowd laughed until the big Indian spoke out strongly, "Me Spotted Horse. My medicine eats bullets," and with that he brought out a big Bowie knife and stabbed it into the bar between the barman's fingers.

In the sudden silence, Spotted Horse licked his big hand, and leaning past Horace, pressed his hand-print beneath the outline of the ace of spades on the dusty blackboard.

"You and me, lady," a short, muscular man next to her said quietly.

"What are you talking about?" she asked, looking at his dark-stubbled face and the knife scar that jagged down the side of his right eye.

"I'll win that shitpot full of money and give it all to you," he murmured matter-of-factly.

"I don't need to ask what's in it for you," she said coldly.

"You give it to me three ways and take that box of money." He shrugged, his eyes fixed on her bosom.

Without waiting for an answer, he yelled to Horace, "Put up Mad Dog Dick O'Toole."

"Dick O'Toole," Horace repeated, and added the name to the list. "You related to Peter O'Dong?"

Again he drew a laugh, and she said plainly, "You're getting yourself killed for nothing. I wouldn't give you a drink of water if you were dried up and blowing away."

"It ain't how a man looks, sweetie." He smiled, showing brown-stained teeth. "It's how he works at it, y'know."

"I know a fuck talker when I hear one," she said disgustedly, and carrying her drink, rose and drifted over to the Kid's table, where he occupied the otherwise empty chair with his boots.

Seeing her coming, the Kid stood up. "Care for a seat, lady?" he asked, wiping the chair seat with his open hand.

"If you can forget about proving your manhood," she said.

"I already proved it so much today, I got nothing left to prove." He grinned wide. "Let me buy you a drink instead."

"A Dead-Eye," she muttered.

As other men called out their names, the Kid made his way to the bar, and after interrupting

Horace at the blackboard to get the drink, returned to the table.

"Scars!" the big tattooed man yelled, and the crowd applauded and called for more.

"Virgil Sparks," a gangly youth with protruding, misshapen teeth called out, and because he looked to be a loser, there was little clapping and more muttering that a kid like him shouldn't degrade the quality of the sport.

The dissent was broken by a half-breed with a sprung leg who yelled out, "Red Buckley, you bastards!"

Before Horace had finished writing, the slim Mexican gunfighter stood and called out, *"Por favor, permiteme. Quiero matar todos de ustedes."*

"You got a name, Mex?"

"Carlos Montoya Castillo de Castillo!" the Mexican called out proudly.

MEX, Horace printed on the blackboard, and looked around for more contestants.

Putting the beer glass nearly full of amber spirits and a floating black olive on the table, the Kid laughed and shook his head. "That Dead-Eye looks to be a real killer. You got hair on your chest?"

"You want this in your face?" she came back at him.

"No, ma'am. I won't make no more jokes about your womanhood," the Kid said soberly. "I think I've got the idea."

"If you do, you're the only one in this whole damn

place," she muttered, and took a solid drink from the beer glass.

"Can I ask what you're doin' here? What you're looking for?"

"It doesn't make any difference. It's just a time and a place. I won't stay."

"But you could if you wanted to?" the Kid asked.

"I guess I could. Why?"

"Town needs new blood. It gets to be plumb boring just talking to jaspers on the run. Always the same old story." The Kid grinned. "He gets off with the strongbox but then ends in the whorehouse, and the next day there's nothing left but a headache and dirty laundry. Then he needs to borrow twenty dollars to go rob another bank."

"What are you doing here?"

"I run the local gun and locksmith store just catty-corner across the street. I'm not exactly sure of my pedigree, but I'm worth three thousand dollars in reward money in four states, and never been convicted of nothing. Folks call me the Kid, and I'm so fast I can get up about noon, rob two trains, a bank, and a stagecoach, shoot the tail feathers off a duck at a hundred yards, and be back to serve you whatever you want before dark."

"That man who did all the shooting from the church? Who was he?"

"Church?" He frowned. "Most everybody forgot it ever was a church," he said thoughtfully. "What do you know about it?"

"Nothing. It has a belfry and a statue. Who's John Herod?"

"Likely he's my daddy, but he don't like to talk about it," the Kid said, grinning again. "He married a young lady that lived here, but then in some mysterious way she got pregnant. He just couldn't believe it, and forty days after I was born and she was able to work, he turned her out."

"Turned her out? You mean he put her on the street?"

"Not on the street." The Kid chuckled ruefully. "Next door."

"But why?" she asked, taking a solid drink from the beer glass.

"Mr. Herod, he don't like to share out much. He likes it the other way."

"You mean he's your father and won't even admit it?" she asked, frowning.

"He's mighty touchy about his private business." The Kid grinned. "He wants to be the biggest he-boar on top the mountain peak."

"But, hell, people grow old, they die. You can't be top dog forever."

"I reckon he'll be dead before Jamboree's over with." The Kid nodded. "He just don't know it yet."

"But he's your father . . . you're his son. . . ." she said, appalled by the idea.

"Let's just say I'm the son of a drummer, or a soldier passing through, say I'm the son of a hundred men who lived here awhile and died sudden like. . . ."

"But you don't believe it."

"No. From what Ma told me, I believe her," the Kid said softly.

"And?"

"Oh, she died years back. The sporters have a lot of fun when they can stand up to it and hold their brandy and their sleeping powders, but once they start downhill, most of 'em will do the Dutch—you know, drink laudanum like you drink Dead-Eyes. Hell, it only takes an ounce to put you to sleep forever." The Kid laughed with moist eyes. "That's why I'm workin' on Mattie, tryin' to get her straightened out some."

"That's a line of bullshit," she said harshly. "I've heard it before."

"Maybe yes, maybe no," he said apologetically. "All you can do is try, right?"

"Just so you stick with her and don't mix me up in it."

"I never knew a lady that had all the answers before. Where you from? Where'd you get the answers?"

"I could be from anywhere, and I got the answers in Madam O'Grady's charm school."

Finishing the drink, she fished out the olive and chewed on it thoughtfully.

"That Herod fellow, he ever come out of his reborn church?"

"Not too often. Everybody that has business with him goes up there, passes through three bodyguards, and talks over the problem."

"So he lives in fear," she said thoughtfully.

"I doubt it. He don't have any fear. He don't have any love, either. He don't have a smile, he don't groan or moan or laugh or kick up his heels or do nothing except tell everybody else what to do."

"Why's he give away a box full of money every year?"

"He don't." The Kid laughed crazily. "He always wins it for himself."

"You mean it's rigged?"

"No. No, the boys wouldn't enter the contest if they had a suspicion it was a setup. It's just he's the fastest there is, except me. . . ." Looking over his shoulder at the bartender, he yelled, "Horace, bring us two Dead-Eyes quick!"

"You may be the fastest gun in Redemption, sonny," she said, "but you sure ain't goin' to drink me under the table and red-dog me."

"Well, I guess the fun is in the tryin'!" The Kid laughed.

Suddenly the raucous laughter and the deafening shouts ceased as if cut off by a knife.

At the bat-wing doors stood a powerful bear of a man dressed in a conservative gray suit of silk and wool, a scarlet watered-silk cravat over a white, starched, pleated shirt. John Herod stood calmly appraising the crowd, then walked toward the bar, his spurs whirring like aroused rattlesnakes.

Bull-shouldered, graying, and not a handsome man, his nose dominated his face and his small mouth disappeared in the hard lines of his cheeks.

His distinct individuality came from his style of walking, his stance, and the diamond hardness of his eyes, which crackled out rays of power to the onlookers.

Used to the display, the Kid chuckled. "That's my pa, the power of darkness."

She froze, paralyzed, forced to take short breaths as she felt the still elegant and powerful nemesis meeting up with the insatiable hatred and fear she felt for the man.

Behind him stood three men in tan dusters, spread out, three sawed-off shotguns at the ready.

"He calls them 'councillors,'" the Kid murmured.

Herod was armed, but careless. The answer to any threat were the councillors standing behind him.

"How many brave men do we have on the list?" Herod asked, pausing beside her, as if to make a point. "I hope there are no eccentric women. . . ."

She stared up at him, thinking she could kill him now, but not survive.

"We got twelve names, Mr. Herod," Horace said. "Thirteen, if you include Flatnose. But him and Ratsy ain't back yet."

"They'll be here," Herod said, moving on to the bar. "They're off running a little errand for me."

"Yes, sir," Horace said.

"Now, let's see what sort of contenders we have," Herod said quietly. "I think I know most of them."

Scanning down the list, Herod frowned and said, "Hanlon. Ace Hanlon, the legendary slayer of seven in one day, albeit a family of mostly children."

"Seven is seven," Ace Hanlon said from his table, not amused.

Herod studied Ace Hanlon's face, his body, and his costume without showing any expression, then turning, he looked at the Kid, frowned, and turned back to the blackboard.

The Kid smiled and shrugged under the malevolent gaze, and under his breath he said, "You see what I mean, sweetie."

Herod read to the end of the list, pursed his thick lips, and said to Horace, "Give me a glass of water."

"Yes, sir," Horace responded quickly.

"That list . . ." Herod murmured, "looks a little scant. Add my name to it, and let's have some fun."

3

SHE STARED AT THE YOKE-SHOULDERED MAN AS HE deliberately exposed his broad back to the room, and she wondered how he could live so long. The world was full of back-shooters looking for a target like that.

But she remembered the three quiet men in long tan dusters. Silently and inconspicuously they had stationed themselves at each end of the bar, and one had stayed by the door, the three effectively covering the whole room with their short shotguns.

How much did he pay them? she wondered. How did he command their loyalty? Usually those closest to the head man were the most dangerous because they either wanted to take over or could be bought.

It was that brute power radiating from him, a force of ruthless authority, that kept him at the top of the heap, a satanic energy that confounded his enemies.

She felt it herself and wondered if she could kill him. Would her hand tremble in fear? Would her eyes fail under his glare? Would her courage match his? Could he be killed at all? Suppose he had an invisible shield surrounding him, the armor of evil incarnate? Something more than a gun had kept him alive. Perhaps it was only that: evil. To use it, to live it, to force it on others, perhaps it was only that force of whole evil that kept everyone else in terror.

Musing over the evil and its personification, she heard two shots in the street and incoherent shouting. The room went quiet until Herod smiled reassuringly and murmured, "That's just Ratsy and Flat Nose. They'll have what I want."

Hardly had he spoken than a tall, powerful man dressed in a rumpled black cleric's suit pitched through the swinging doors. His hands were tied in front and he had no way of stopping himself from falling and sliding through the dirty sawdust to the foot of the bar.

"Sonofabitch put up a hell of a fight," Flat Nose said, coming in the doorway.

Flat Nose was so named because his nose looked as if someone had flattened it with a rolling pin, forcing him to breathe through his mouth and to snuffle.

Behind him a smaller ferret-faced man with furtive eyes and receding chin followed.

"He don't never want to quit," Ratsy said in a deep voice that belied his stature. "You can club him down, but he don't learn."

The captive rolled over and sat with his back to the bar, showing a reversed white collar over his black vest. Although bound and beaten, he still maintained the quiet dignity of a pastor.

"Well, hello, Cort," the spectral Herod greeted the minister warmly. "I was beginning to wonder if you were going to make it in time." Smiling, he added, "You shouldn't stay away so long, old friend."

Cort stared at Herod as if in some way he could give the big man mercy, kindness, compassion, but Herod failed to notice.

"I hear you started a mission down in Hermosillo. That right?" Herod smiled. "Your own little piece of heaven? Sunlight and yellow cactus flowers, you and your little ragged orphans praying for all the lost souls . . ."

"We burned down the damn mission like you said, Mr. Herod," Ratsy said with a grin on his back-sloped face, and as Herod chuckled, others in the room relaxed and laughed along with him.

Cort stared around the room, unable to contain or hide his loathing for his persecutors. Still he would not speak.

Herod took a sip of water, set the glass down, and like a cat toying with a mouse, shook his head sadly and said, "All that work, Cort, all those years of hardship, just destroyed for no reason at all. That must bother you some."

Cort didn't acknowledge the mocking nor the taunting smile.

"My, we used to have us some times, Cort." Herod

smiled, remembering and thinking back. "'Course you was just a kid when I took you in and taught you everything you know . . . then you just had to get uppity . . . wanting to change things. . . ."

"You'll never change," Cort said quietly. "You could, but you won't."

"Likely that's the difference between us, Cort. I won't change, but you will." Herod quit playing.

As Cort shook his head, not in defiance, but in simple denial, Herod sipped from the water glass and spoke harshly. "You used to be fast as a cut cat. Are you still fast?"

Cort didn't reply. Instead he closed his eyes, perhaps from simple weariness, perhaps in silent prayer.

"Don't go to sleep on me now, Cort," Herod growled. "I asked you if you were still fast."

Angrily, Herod glared at the younger man and asked sharply, "Don't I even get an answer? You take a damnfool vow of silence or something?"

The expression on Cort's face remained serene, and his eyes remained closed.

"I said, are you still fast?"

Suddenly in a rage, Herod threw a glass of water at Cort's head.

She saw the glass leave Herod's hand, and then in a blur, Cort's body shift, his hands no longer between his legs, but extended and holding the half-full glass of water.

The awestruck crowd sighed in disbelief as Cort put the glass to his lips and drank it dry.

Putting the glass carefully on the floor, Cort murmured, "Faster than you, John, but I won't fight in your Jamboree."

A horrible smile lighted Herod's heavy features, and he said flatly, "We'll see about that."

Turning to Ratsy, Herod said, "String him up."

"Outside?" Ratsy said eagerly.

"No, in here," Herod snapped. "Put him on a chair."

Horrorstruck, she watched Flat Nose grab Cort under the arms and lift him onto a chair as Ratsy threw the end of a rope over a hook screwed into the ceiling, fashioned a hangman's noose, and slipped it over Cort's head.

Drawing the noose tightly around Cort's neck so that the long knot lay snugly under Cort's right ear, Ratsy passed the other end of the rope around the brass foot rail, drew it tight so that Cort was standing on the chair tiptoe, then secured it with a double half hitch.

"Nicely done, Ratsy. You're a natural-born hangman," Herod said.

There was a scramble of townspeople leaving their tables and heading for the door.

They can't bear to see a preacher hung, she thought, but they won't do anything to stop it, either. No one will stand up against the evil, no one will interfere, and God in his inscrutable way will let His servant strangle to death.

More merciful to put a bullet between his eyes.

She felt like screaming NO, NO, NO, and at the same time laying her face on her arm and weeping.

Who was this clergyman defying the power of darkness? What had he been to the other? Where was love and respect, beauty and laughter? Where had they all gone? Or were they inside the tall man in the shabby black coat?

Watching him, she thought she saw in his face all the goodness and joy of mankind there, as well as the acknowledgment of its hatred and misery. She thought she could see that he had shared in the lowest of abominations, yet serenely sought the highest virtue of the human soul. She believed then that here was a man who had *changed* himself. In that knowing, she was seduced by grace.

Slipping his gold-plated Peacemaker free of its hard leather holster, Herod brought the hammer back to full cock, and with the barrel pointed at the ceiling, he said levelly, "Think about it, Cort."

Suddenly, Herod's arm snapped forward like a rattler striking and flame bloomed from his hand.

The bullet smashed a leg of the chair and thunked into the front of the bar.

"You're dead wrong, Cort," Herod said. "You're not near as good as you think."

Cort looked down at the big man and said softly, "But I am not evil anymore."

"A skunk can't change his stripe," Herod replied, and snapped his hand forward again. The blast shook the room, and a second chair leg disintegrated.

"Change your mind, Cort. Remember how it was when we shared the danger and the money, the blood and the killing, the good golden brandy and always the willing women. . . ."

"You know when I changed my mind," Cort spoke tiredly. "I'm not changing it back."

She heard the chair creak and sway as Cort balanced his weight. She saw the hard resolve in his face, hard planes of experience, bleak angles welded into stubborn rectitude, and she wondered if he'd accept death before compromise.

"You're not thinking straight yet, Cort." Again Herod's arm lashed out and his hand stabbed forward, releasing the thunderbolt.

Silently, their guts sucked in, the audience watched spellbound.

The chair swayed on one leg as Cort struggled to find the new balance.

"Go ahead, Herod. You know I'm past begging."

"This is your last chance, Cort." Herod shrugged. "It's yes or no. It's kill or be killed. It's hope or maggot bait."

Slowly, Herod settled the Peacemaker's sights on the fourth chair leg, waiting for an answer.

Hardly aware that she was standing, let alone speaking out, she murmured into the vast silence, "Put my name up."

Every eye in the room turned to look at her. Horace stared with his mouth open and stammered, "There is no women allowed in the quick draw. It's a rule."

Herod looked at her with new interest. He had no recollection of her as he lazily undressed her with his eyes, and liking what he saw, he let his gaze linger on her, fondle her.

Cort looked at her in a different way. Questioning, with a note of hope or despair, it all depended on what she was inside. He could only hope for the best.

The chair cracked ominously and Horace looked over at Herod. "That's right, ain't it, Mr. Herod?"

"There are no rules that prohibit ladies from entering the contest. It's just that females can't shoot for shit," Herod growled.

Turning back toward Cort, he said heatedly, "I'm tired of this. I'll make up your mind for you, maggot bait."

Again the golden six-gun arced downward, and as the hammer fell, the fourth chair leg shattered, letting the chair fall away from the hanging man.

Still on her feet, she felt her hand drop to the Colt .44 as if she had nothing to do with it, as if she were a bystander watching a strongly built woman neatly, with no wasted motion, clearing leather, pointing the weapon, and with the heel of her left hand fanning off three shots so fast they sounded like one.

Good shooting, she thought—whoever you are. . . .

The tight-stretched hemp parted and the hanging man dropped heavily to the floor.

The three men in tan dusters had their short greeners aimed at her, and taking a deep breath, she calmly holstered her weapon.

Her bullets had ricocheted into the bottles on the shelves behind the bar, splattering Horace with broken glass and white lightning.

His daughter Katie stood beside him staring at the lady in golden buckskins, her eyes rounded with wonder.

The men in tan dusters waited for a command, and Herod very nearly gave them the nod they wanted, but he held back his anger, instinctively thinking there was more here than he could see, and if she were dead, he'd never find out what it was. For sure, he wanted to know, he had to know. Once he was certain about who she was and what she was doing in his town, she could die or disappear into Eugene Dred's whorehouse, it wouldn't make much difference.

Suddenly, the anger twisting his heavy features vanished and he laughed at the ridiculous incongruity of the scene, a damn woman upstaging him, taking the play away from him, cheating him, in a way, of his bloody prey and satisfaction.

"Oh, hell," he said, regaining his poise and holding a broad smile, "put them both in the contest."

Horace started to comply, then, puzzled, looked at her and asked, "What's your name, ma'am?"

"Smith," she said, and settled down in her chair.

The Kid was the only one to laugh.

As the clock tolled, Horace cocked his head, listening for a moment, then yelled, "It's midnight! The entry board is closed. Free drinks for the fighters and may the best man . . . woman . . . shootist win! Let's hear a cheer for Mr. Herod!"

The few townspeople remaining scurried out the door and made for the safety of their homes as the crowd of gunmen pushed out into the street and commenced firing their weapons at the stars, a hundred heavy caliber guns roaring in the night, accompanied by the squalling, hooting, high-pitched Apache screams of desperate men on a tear.

The primitive, thunderous cacophony continued until their guns were emptied, and she saw their faces radiant with a rutting excitement, as if they'd already tasted blood and craved more.

"Here's you another Dead-Eye," the Kid said.

"You have one too?" she asked.

"You wouldn't care nothing about me if I didn't, would you?" The Kid grinned and lifted his glass to touch hers.

"Why would I care anything about you?" she asked, taking a drink.

"'Cause I'm such a likable little cuss." The Kid laughed. "Once you get to know me real well, I'll have to throw rocks at you to keep you off me."

"Sorry, Kid," she said, setting aside her empty glass, "drink her down or quit fooling around."

"So if I drink her down can I fool around?" the Kid asked, emptying his glass and heading back inside the saloon for a refill.

"Little cuss," she said to his back, "you drink with me, you won't even feel like fooling around."

* * *

She felt the dry scum in her mouth, and then the pile driver slammed in her head, splitting her skull, crashing her brain. She opened one eye and groaned, and closed the eye as her brain ball mashed flat again.

Wet with sweat, she wondered what horror she'd been dreaming about. Whatever it was would be better than this stupendous excrucilation inside her skull, yet there was no going back. She already knew what the dream was, but she was ashamed that she couldn't exorcise it, burn it out of the child's brain, hawk it up and spit it back into a time when she had not existed. Some way, somehow, put it behind and lose it forever.

Even then, with a blinding hangover, she glimpsed the shining forehead with the blue-red hole centered in it.

Opening her eyes, she suddenly felt overwhelmed by guns. Guns of every make and caliber, guns of every design and hard metal, guns old and new, single-shooters, double-shooters, five-shooters, pepperboxes, and six-shooters. Over and unders, and side by sides, and four-barreled guns. Walled in by guns, she began to think she was dreaming again or had been poisoned.

What wasn't full of guns was full of locks and masses of keys. Brass, steel, bronze, cast iron, big and small, old and new.

"I'm dying," she said, feeling the rough blankets against her bare skin. Opening her eyes again, she saw a framed picture already brown with age of a beautiful blond-haired boy about six years old. He strained to hold two six-guns in the air and around his slim chest were two bandoliers full of cartridges.

"Sweetheart, did I hear you calling my name?" came the voice of the Kid.

"Glass of water, please," she muttered, closing her eyes again.

"To the rescue," the Kid said, standing by the makeshift bed with a glass of water in one hand and a Root side-hammer revolver in the other.

Taking a gulp of water, she swished it around her mouth and spewed it out on the floor.

"That's better," she said weakly, and drank the rest.

The Kid settled down in a chair and commenced stripping the old Root .31 caliber down and wiping each piece with an oily rag even as he watched her.

"Where am I?" she asked, looking around at all the guns on the walls.

"My place. Redemption Gun Store. 'Straight Shooter' is my motto."

"It's coming back to me," she muttered, touching her naked hips surreptitiously.

"You want some breakfast, little wifie-pie?" The Kid grinned at her as he reassembled the old pistol. "Or would you like some more of what you had last night?"

She stared at him, shook her head in dismissal and closed her eyes again.

"If you can't remember what all happened, I'll

gladly fill you in." The Kid grinned like a cat full of canary.

"Oh, Christ," she said, keeping her eyes closed and feeling the maul slowly beating her brains into scrambled eggs.

Thinking about scrambled eggs, she wanted to puke, but she couldn't shame herself in front of the Kid, and that led to another remembrance that cheered her up some.

"I was at my best," the Kid said softly, his eyes shining lovingly, "and you were like a young mare. . . ."

"By God, you've got a brag a mile wide," she said, opening one eye.

"I'll never forget that scream of yours when I hit bottom." He smiled, shaking his head in fond remembrance.

"How'd I get here?" she muttered.

"We was adrinkin' those Dead-Eyes, and you topped me in the drinking contest and then I kind of topped you in the bare ass department."

"Kid," she said huskily, "you're welcome to your bullshit dream, and I recall you throwing up your guts in the street and passing out under the horse trough, so let's not be making any plans for a baby shower, okay?"

The Kid grinned and said, "It ain't too late to try right now."

"Wrong again," she said crossly, closing her eyes again, hoping for a blissful nap, but beneath the single blanket the bed was rock hard and not exactly flat.

Opening her eyes, she asked, "Goddamn it, how can you sleep on this? It's like lying on a brick staircase. . . ."

"I know," the Kid said sorrowfully, "but the way this town is, I got to sleep on it or the sonsabitches will steal it."

Shaking her head, she rolled over on her side, lifted the bottom blanket and read the stenciled label on one of the boxes.

> DANGER
> HANDLE WITH CARE
> DYNAMITE
> E.I. Dupont & Co.

"Jesus Christ, I'm glad I slept alone. There's studs could set this off with just fooling around."

He smiled. "Now you're bragging."

"Well—I can dream." She grinned at him.

"You don't belong here," he said quietly, dry-firing the old Root.

"Where do I belong?" she asked, bored already.

"You ought to be home boiling oatmeal and tending to the kids."

"Get it out of your head, Kid. Our world isn't like that. I don't want a frame house and a parlor and kids. I want to shoot somebody."

"Today's the day." He shrugged. "Who you goin' to call out?"

"Herod."

"I wouldn't do that if I was you," he said, setting the Root aside and taking his own Smith & Wesson from its holster. "He'll kill you quicker'n owl shit. I mean he don't care, man, woman, or child."

"Fine with me. I don't want anybody telling me I'm too demure to pull a trigger."

"It ain't you're so demure, it's that you ought to be motherin' kids like I was once," the Kid said, dropping the brass-cased cartridges into his hand. "Men's men. Women's women. Men is fathers, women is mothers, see?"

"And black widow spiders are still spinning their webs." She chuckled. "You got to learn that the female mind is unscrupulously immoral and deadly."

"I can see you been through a lot. Even if I don't understand you, I still feel the wrong that's hidin' under all that hard talk."

"Kid, we're not made for each other," she said crossly, throwing the blanket aside and reaching for her pants.

"You're better built than I figured," the Kid said. "Marry me."

"Herod," she said. "I'm here to kill him. After that we talk about washing diapers."

"Lady, there's some things I'm more expert on than you, and one of 'em is Herod. The true fact is I'm about the only jasper in town could stand up to him, and I'm in no hurry to try."

"Why not?" she asked, buttoning up her shirt.

"Hell, he's my father."

"Does he recognize you as his son?" she challenged him.

"Sometimes." The Kid shrugged. "I mean, I wish he would. Or I wish someone would. It's not right being in doubt, because you want to look up to somebody."

"Sure," she said sympathetically, "but at least you don't hate it all. Count your blessings."

"I don't hate nothing. And I don't need for nothing." He grinned. "I sure like the way you slip into your clothes so natural like."

"They wean kids too soon. Damn men, they never get over bein' short-titted." She grinned at him. "Grown men, still they got to suck tit to fuck. Wolves aren't that way. Coyotes aren't that way. Even rabbits aren't that way. Once they're done sucking, they're done."

"Jesus God, you're a hard woman," the Kid said shakily. "What the hell is scratchin' you?"

"From Redemption to Butcher Town," she said softly. "I didn't ask for the trip, but I was sent anyways."

"Honey . . . punkin pie . . ." the Kid said sympathetically.

"Save it," she said curtly, angry at herself for being a blabbermouth. "What's for breakfast?"

"Tequila." He chuckled and tossed a pint bottle of clear liquor to her.

Catching it with her left hand, she pulled the cork

and smelled the liquor. "Smells homemade." She nodded and tilted the bottle to her lips.

Pushing the cork back in the bottle, she said with misty eyes, "God, that's good. . . ."

The Kid stared bug-eyed at her.

"What the hell?" she snapped. "You never seen a woman fire a six-shooter fast? You never seen a naked woman dress? You never seen a woman drink tequila in the morning?"

"There's Ira's Worrisome Eats down the street," he said, backing away. "Old Ira can fry up some pretty good mountain oysters and eggs."

"That's what I need," she said fiercely, feeling the tequila sweeten her blood. "Fried bull's balls, and lots of 'em."

After carefully locking the front door, the Kid escorted her down the street a half block to the dimly lighted café. As they walked along, anonymous whistles sounded, and sotto voce voices. ". . . I'd sure slap the old wagon tongue to her. . . ." ". . . If'n he long-cocked her, she don't show it. . . ." "Suppose she charges?" "I bet his pecker is rawed and wrapped in cotton. . . ."

Bleary-eyed gunmen drifted out onto the street, touchy, scratchy, dangerous as rattlesnakes in August when they shed their skins and strike blindly at any contrary vibration or heat distortion.

Up ahead of them she saw two gunsels, sleepy-eyed and hung over, blunder into each other, and still touching each other, each drew and fired point-blank.

Cotton shirts burned, blood flooded from their midsections as they fell, and she thought, The damn fools never even woke up.

She saw Scars lounging back in a chair on the veranda of the whorehouse, looking sour as pickled brisket.

"Look at the pair of turtle doves," he muttered.

"Good morning," she said.

"I'll bet you broke his back and made him bleed," Scars snarled at her.

"You'll never know, will you, Scars?" she said, smiling enigmatically.

4

CARLOS MONTOYA AND VIRGIL SPARKS GLARED AT
each other, trying to make the other blink or look
away. Sparks blinked but he did not look away. Other
gunfighters paced on the boardwalk, trying to relax.

Wearing his big Texas hat, Sparks leaned back
against the fire house wall, clanking coins in his right
hand, keeping his fingers loose and supple.

Gutzon, the long-faced Swede, prowled up and
down the middle of the street, a ferocious scowl on
his pale Nordic face. He carried a polished mahogany box close to his chest, as if someone might steal
his most prized possession. He called the box his
armory, because it contained a finely crafted, long-
barreled Swiss Neuhausen dueling pistol, ammunition, cleaning brushes, rags, and a screwdriver, as
well as a number of medals for marksmanship.

The blind boy emerged from the alley, feeling his

way with his left hand on the old bank wall and pulling his wheeled trunk with his right hand. Arriving at the front porch of the saloon, he opened the lid, which in turn lifted up tiers of trays filled with small miscellanea.

In the main square between the saloon and the Kid's gun shop was the town well and water trough, equipped with a hand pump available to all.

Fettered to an iron hitching ring at the end of the trough, the tall cleric, Cort, squatted uncomfortably. He'd been chained there all night.

Rising, slopping water on his face, he shook his head and dried off with his sleeves. Up and down the street he saw that the townspeople, furtive as gray rats, were setting up chairs on the boardwalk, getting ready for the big day.

Looking over at old Hiram Whiteside, Cort called out, "There's a bad smell stinking up this town. It's been getting worse and worse."

Whiteside pretended not to hear, but a Mexican girl came to pump a bucket of water, and she took her time, listening.

"You know what it is?" Cort continued. "It's fear, terror. You all been here so long, you can't smell it anymore."

An old man paused as he crossed the street, stared at Cort and listened, but Virgil Sparks moved over and muttered, "Get your ass movin', old man."

The old man flinched, and humbled, bowed his head and hurried on.

"Herod's just one man! You think he can't be beaten? He can, and I'll help you do it. . . ."

Montoya saw the Mexican girl dawdling, and snapped out, *"Apurate!"* and she, too, jerked back into reality and hurried off with her bucket of water.

"It only needs one of you to help get these chains off," Cort held on, his voice rising and falling with conviction. "Then we'll face him together. What do you say?"

His answer was an apple core thrown at his head, and as he turned to see where it came from, Flat Nose stepped close and kicked him in the ribs, sending the tall prisoner sprawling facedown on the ground.

"Shut your goddamn mouth," Flat Nose growled indignantly. "You'll wake up my boss."

Cort wiped the dirt off his face with his sleeve. An expression of livid, lethal rage passed quickly, and by the time he faced Flat Nose, his features were once again serene, and he said quietly, "God is a righteous judge, strong and patient; and God is provoked every day.'"

Behind Flat Nose, Cort saw five ragged and unwashed boys standing warily poised to run if he should turn and strike out. They bore bruises and lumps that testified to their father's quickness, and they carried pieces of stove wood.

"Meet my family, preacher," Flat Nose snuffled. "I done learned 'em to hate everybody . . . especially an uppity do-gooder."

"You deserve better," Cort said to the street urchins.

"You been challenged to fight in the Jamboree yet?" Flat Nose asked carelessly.

"I'm not fighting you or anyone else for the entertainment of John Herod."

"I'll go get us a time," Flat Nose said, grinning, "while you tell my boys all about Moses in the bulrushes. They don't get to Sunday school much."

Leaving Cort encircled by the ratty pack of kids, Flat Nose strolled off toward the saloon.

The oldest boy, with shaggy matted hair, yelled at Cort, "He's goin' to kill you, preacher, you do-gooder bastard!"

Scuttling forward, he hit Cort on the shoulder with his billet of wood and darted back fearfully. Turning to his brothers, he yipped, "Hit the sonofabitch! Kick him, make him bawl like a baby!"

She saw Flat Nose shuffle off toward the saloon, saw the boys nerve themselves up to attack the manacled man, but before she could cross over to the water trough, Charlie Moonlight drove his black-painted cart in front of her on his way out of town.

She saw the pinewood coffin in the back and asked, "Who's in there?"

"I dunno." Moonlight smiled at her. "The boys called him Slow Show, and they was right sure enough."

By the time the way was clear, she saw the tall man down on one knee, trying to protect his head and neck from the boys' abuse.

Leaping like a tigress, she grabbed the biggest boy by the hair and threw him head first against the trough. The second she clouted with a backhand, and the third she kicked in the butt, sending him sailing. Suddenly the urchins scattered like quail.

Looking down at Cort, she asked, "Sleep well?"

"At least I slept alone," he replied steadily, and she caught the veiled accusation.

"You don't know nothing, do you?" she came back at him. "You sound like just another sour-faced, narrow-minded hypocrite."

"I'm trying to do some good. Preach peace."

"You find a tribe of contented Indians and you make 'em wear clothes," she snapped. "Then after you baptize them, you kill 'em with smallpox and send them all up to your properly dressed heaven."

"I know," he said humbly, "it used to be that way, but it's not my way."

"What is your way, then?"

"If I could just educate the poor so they could defend themselves against the rich . . . if I could just do that, I'd be satisfied."

"You're wasting your time." She shook her head.

"Don't put me down any lower than I feel," Cort said. "I'm tired of it."

"In case you forgot, preacher," she came back at him, "I saved your life last night."

"You just stretched it out a speck." Cort got to his feet. "It's not important."

"You sound like a quitter," she said, trying to figure him out. There he stood, a physically powerful man, yet meek as a lamb, like mustard without the bite. "These bastards burn down your mission, chain you up, kick you around like a yeller dog—don't you want to fight back?"

"Of course I do," Cort said quietly. "I'd like to send them to hell for what they've done, but even if I could, I won't. Killing people is wrong. It goes against the Good Book. . . ."

"I heard that sermon already," she cut him off. "I just wonder if you're an entire man—"

Over Cort's shoulder she saw Herod coming down the stairway of his mansion and pass by the marble statue. His three councillors covered him on either side and the rear as he strode like an emperor down the street. Dressed in a freshly pressed black suit and an ermine-trimmed cloak to ward off the morning chill, his elegance also declared he was the most important power in town.

". . . like him," she added, and headed back to the saloon.

Herod was there ahead of her, his rear guard walking backward with his shotgun at the ready, watching her, and anyone else who might have back-shooting intentions.

As she came to the bat-wing doors, she was puzzled by the silence. She heard a fly buzzing against a windowpane. She heard the creak of the bat-wing doors as she pushed through, and she saw Herod at the far end of the bar, his holstered gold-plated revolvers flashing like sunshine, and he was sipping a glass of water.

Horace, the bartender, was down at the other end of the bar counting out money from the till into two piles while one of the bodyguards watched. When the till was empty and the money divided equally, Horace reluctantly pushed one pile toward the councillor and put the rest in his pocket.

Herod's back was exposed as she slowly crossed the room, her face as hard as a horseshoe, concealing the confused fear she felt rising in her throat.

Sergeant Quanson, sitting at a table pretending to be reading a paper, glanced up and caught her eyes. He read the wish, but doubted her courage.

Moving on, she approached Herod's back. Her hands were sweating and she wondered if her boots were dragging. Something kept telling her to wait, now was not the best time. He had a trick or two up his sleeve. Under that cape maybe he wore boiler-plate armor.

Torn between the opportunity to cold-bloodedly back-shoot the man she had come to kill, she hesitated, and before she could make her move, a hand smelling of shit grabbed her by the shoulder.

"You're mine!" came the triumphant howl of Dog Kelly.

Freezing her sudden fear and dismay, she slowly turned to face the bushwhacker from the desert.

Still handcuffed to a chunk of wood that he had finally broken loose from the tree stump, he glared at her with his deranged, inflamed eyes, lusting for revenge. His face was pink as a baby's bottom, and the skin was peeling off in strips like wood shavings.

"I put your name up, Mr. Kelly, I knew you'd get here!" Horace said warmly.

Not changing expression, Kelly snarled, "I challenge you, you rotten bitch!"

"I'm not fighting you. You're crazy."

"You ain't got a choice!" Dog Kelly shouted triumphantly, as if he'd turned over his hole card and filled out four aces.

"I said—" she started to repeat herself, but Herod abruptly turned to face her.

"What are you doing here?" he demanded, his voice harsh and coercive.

She stood still, facing him unflinchingly, and tried to stare him down, but she was afraid and she knew it. The power that emanated from his burly, bull-shouldered person overwhelmed her resolve, and she was left to hiding her trembling nerves.

"I came to win the money." She lied well because she'd expected the question.

Still he doubted her, perhaps because he had rehearsed the scene more thoroughly in his mind than she had.

Backing up against the bar, he looked her up and down, taking his time making his mind up.

"The rules are clear. You cannot refuse a challenge," he said judiciously, a small smile on his wide mouth. "You don't like the rules, now's the time to back away and dust on out of town."

"I'll go by the rules," she said tautly, refusing to back down from him.

Horace from behind the bar called out, "The lady fights Mr. Kelly! And they fight at . . ." He brought an old top hat from behind the bar and pulled a slip of paper out. Waving it around for all to see, he added, ". . . at seven o'clock tonight!"

John Herod studied her face a moment longer, daring her to speak up, announce her intentions, get her secret off her chest, but she somberly returned his gaze and asked, "Satisfied, Mr. Herod?"

"It'll take more than that to satisfy me," Herod said, finishing his glass of water.

"What would it take?" She asked the obvious question with a trace of contempt.

Herod looked at her again, and said, "If you will excuse me, please, I am going to challenge the most dangerous man in town."

As Herod strode toward the front door, Horace studied the blackboard and called after him, "First fight starts at noon, Mr. Herod."

Angry with herself for having quailed before the man she hated, she shook her head, took a deep breath, and went back outside.

Sidling down the boardwalk, she saw at the end of the street Ace Hanlon making a show for the locals and a few bored gunmen. Spreading out a deck of cards in a fan, he turned to a small, eager girl. "Take a card, little sweetheart—any card."

The little girl obligingly picked out a card and stared perplexedly at Ace Hanlon's back as he walked away.

"Hold it up for all the folks to see!" Ace called to her without turning around. As the girl lifted the card over her head, Ace Hanlon's right hand stabbed to the butt of his gleaming Colt, brought it up across his chest and fired over his left shoulder.

The little girl screamed in terror as the bullet snapped through the card an inch from her fingers.

Turning, Ace said mockingly to the frightened girl, "Ace of spades."

She held up the card for him to see. It was the ace of spades with a hole through it, dead center.

The crowd cheered and broke into applause and Ace Hanlon looked at them as if they were lesser beings applauding the Sun God, then bowed courteously and holstered the revolver.

The applause ceased abruptly when Herod stepped forward and said coldly, "That's a neat card trick. Didn't you blow the thumb off a little girl in Las Cruces practicing that same stunt?"

Ace Hanlon shook his head contemptuously and said, "You're all smudge and no fire, Herod."

"Ask Horace to pick us out a good time to meet, then we'll see what's cool blue smoke and what's fire."

"I'm the best and the last you'll ever see." Ace Hanlon eyed Herod coldly as if from a mountain top.

"Put an ace in your shirt pocket, Hanlon," Herod growled impassively. "I'll teach you a card trick you've never seen before."

Before Hanlon could reply, John Herod turned on

his heel and strode back to his winged mansion at the head of the street.

The minute hand lacked three minutes from catching up with the hour hand already standing at twelve on the town clock.

Where there had been scarcely twenty people on the street an hour before, now there were close to two hundred. The balcony of the saloon was crowded to overflowing, and youngsters perched on roofs in order to get a better view of the dueling ground.

The glaring overhead sun made the street blisteringly hot, and the festive crowd fanned themselves with palm fronds and folded-up newspapers.

On the street, Charlie Moonlight, like an ominous rubbish collector, waited by his cart, his dark hand resting on a newly finished coffin. Near him a photographer sat up his apparatus, and beside him stood old Doc Wallace, black bag dangling from his shaky, arthritic hand.

Flags drooped from ropes stretched across the street, but there was an air of tension, an expectancy of a violent death struggle, and all business in the town had come to a standstill.

A housewife in faded calico ran out into the street, grabbed up her small child and ran back to her house. Iron shutters barred the store windows from stray bullets. People checked their watches as the great town clock rasped in its innards and ticked off another minute.

Pockmarked Eugene Dred sat on one of a half-dozen velvet-covered chairs on the veranda of his whorehouse, surrounded by his raucous harem dressed in all their transcendent finery.

Beckoning to Scars, he whispered in the tattooed man's ruined ear, "Put this two hundred on Gutzon. Maybe it'll give him a little more confidence."

"Two hundred on Gutzon," Scars repeated, taking the money and going off to find one of the Kid's supporters. He reckoned Dred was making the crazy bet because he wanted the Kid eliminated before he had to fight him.

Working it out slowly in his head, Scars decided to pocket the money and save everybody a lot of trouble.

Sergeant Quanson sat on a chair next to the shoeshine stand, his head back against the wall, his eyes closed as if he were asleep.

In front of the corner Volunteer Fire Department, Herod lolled back alone on a cast-iron bench, with Cort, still manacled, crouching at his feet. Herod idly puffed on a long black cigar and nudged Cort in the ribs with his right spur.

"Nice day for the Jamboree," Herod said conversationally.

"You could be doing something better with your time," Cort said quietly.

"You against blood sport, too?" Herod chuckled. "Hell, I remember how you danced a jig when you beat Cal Cunningham to the draw."

At one end of the street she saw Gutzon opening his carved mahogany box containing the immaculate

Neuhausen .45. He appeared to be businesslike, turgid, but efficient, ready to pick up the prize money and take it back to Sweden.

At the other end of the street, almost in front of her, the Kid practiced twirling his twin Schofields, up and down, from one hand to the other like a demented magician juggling mirrors. Back and forth he paced, his guns flashing in the air, a cocky smile on his wide open face.

He nodded at her as he came near, then turned and strolled toward Mattie Silk, sitting near Eugene Dred. Orbiting the Schofields around his trigger fingers, he bowed to her and she blew a kiss back at him.

"You're next, Eugene," he called out to Dred, who glared at him.

"I just bet two hundred dollars that you'll be dead within ninety seconds," Dred sneered.

Moving back to his station, the Kid eyed the clock and heard the rasping gear bring the minute hand up to one minute of twelve.

Horace strode importantly out into the middle of the street and announced, "Gents, remember, you must not draw until the clock makes the first chime of the hour."

"What happens if a man gets excited and shoots early?" the Kid hooted, grinning at the crowd.

"Then they're cheats." Herod stood and spoke loudly. "And they'll be eliminated from the competition."

From the rooftops came the snick of three separate

levers loading and cocking the Winchesters held by the men in tan dusters.

She understood immediately what Herod meant by eliminated.

Horace glanced up at the great clock and continued with the rules. "You must continue firing until one man is down. Whoever is left standing is the winner. Take your positions, gents, the street is now yours."

"Please, boy," Gutzon shouted, "I will only wound you in the foot so you can lose gracefully."

"Whoo-ee!" the Kid hooted. "You're the dumbest damn squarehead I ever seen! Don't be too kind. I don't deserve it!"

She watched the two men square up and wait for the first chime.

She looked over at Cort and saw that he was transfixed, as intense as anyone in the crowd. Above him, Herod watched closely, tossed his cigar away and licked his lips.

She heard the spring unwind a fraction and the gear creak, and as the minute hand snapped vertically, the first chime struck. Gutzon went for his gun, catching the Kid clowning with his hands going the wrong way at the crucial moment.

As the Swede's long, sleek gun came up, the Kid accelerated his draw and his bullet socked into Gutzon's shoulder, spinning him around before the Swede could even get off a round.

As Gutzon stared dumbly in amazement, the Kid

turned to the crowd, did a dazzling twirl and a double border shift, strutted cockily in a little circle like a fighting rooster, and cried out, "Have you ever seen such a thing? I'm the phantom tornado crossed on a spring steel trap and a redheaded woodpecker! Whoo-ee! Damn, I am fast!"

As the Kid howled out his own joyful praise, Gutzon regained control and stolidly reckoned that he still had a chance.

Raising his Neuhausen to aim at the Kid's profiled side, he set himself and aimed carefully. Quickly the Kid whirled a step to the left and sent his ball into Gutzon's thigh.

Gutzon still stood stoically, but his revolver pointed at the ground.

"Hey, Mr. Swedish Champion! Are you done yet? You got to get down on at least one knee or I got to shoot you again!"

Gutzon's tall frame bent to the ground. He laid the pistol aside and knelt on one knee as if kneeling before his master with his head bowed in defeat.

Doc Wallace grimly walked over and, bending over him, opened the black bag and poked around inside.

"Kid's winner!" Horace yelled, leaping out to the Kid and holding his right hand up high.

The crowd squalled like Comanches, applauding as the Kid did his little circular strut and laughingly yelled, "Was I fast or is Sweden just a place where they never thaw out? Was I fast? Was I faster'n chain lightning with a link napped? Was I fast as a bat outta hell with his tail afire? Did you ever *see* me, I was so fast? Whoo-ee!"

She couldn't help but smile at the Kid's comedy, but she saw John Herod out of the corner of her eye jerk Cort's chain and taunt him. "How does it feel, Cort? Remind you of the good times? Makes your heart beat faster and your blood frothy? Sure it does."

Her gaze returned to the skylarking Kid doing his little dance again, when the photographer's flash powder exploded and the lens clicked, recording the moment perhaps forever.

Mattie Silk ran down the steps and gave the Kid a big hug and a hard kiss on the mouth.

The Kid looked over at Herod and grinned, expecting a few words of approval, but instead receiving a withering look that stopped the celebration dead.

Standing, Herod said disgustedly, "Fast? Hell's fire, if the squarehead'd been any slower, he'd have had robins nesting on his hat and birdshit on his nose. You should have killed him the first shot."

The Kid's smile faded and his mouth turned surly. "What's the matter with you? Why kill him?"

"This is a man's game, Kid," Herod said balefully. "You want to play with tin soldiers and china dolls, you better play someplace else."

Looking down at Cort, the Kid asked anxiously,

"What's the matter with him? You've known him longer'n anybody. Was he always like this?"

"Yes," Cort said, "always had to be top dog. He wasn't born to it, but he learned it early."

"Listen to the preacher," Herod said coldly. "He don't remember the proverb, 'He that hideth hatred is of lying lips' . . . and that's why I've always been faster than anybody else, because I never tried to hide anything."

"What's the matter with folks just having a good time?" the Kid asked, shaking his head.

"Can't you learn, Kid, that the biggest belly laugh in the world comes when you kill a man? It doesn't have to be face-to-face. You can shoot him in the back from four hundred yards and you'll still feel like laughin' your head off at how you topped him," Herod said like a patient teacher talking to the third-grade dunce.

"I don't feel that way," the Kid said. "I'm a shooter, but not a killer."

"He can't help it, Kid," Cort said. "He won't be happy until he makes this place pure hell."

"Listen to him! A dust-bin orphan, hungry, cold, gut-shrunk, ragged-ass and afoot. I fed him, clothed him, and gave him a gun. He was doing pretty good . . ." Herod paused and frowned. ". . . and then he backslid and tried to run out on me."

"Why did he backslide?" the Kid asked.

"You don't need to know, Kid," Cort said quickly. "Just figure the slaughter of innocents gave me a bellyache."

"Why can't you talk plain out?" The Kid looked from one man to the other. "Was it all so bad you can't even cough it up?"

"Yes," Cort said, his voice hollow and trembling. Looking up heavenward as if for help, he saw her standing there, listening.

5

SHE HAD COME TO KILL HIM, BUT SHE'D FAILED, BEtrayed by a primitive fear that cowered before his dominance. Now she'd fallen into a competition that changed her course and diluted her resolve. She'd become another one of his pawns without ever daring to challenge him.

It could not go on this way, she decided, coming down the stairs from her room to the front porch of the saloon. I've got to take the initiative. I've got to force the fight. I've got to kill him before somebody else does.

I cannot leave here so long as he lives, she thought, and yet I have to crack that inhuman armor first. If he figures out what I want, he'll simply order me killed while he's up at his big house having tea and crumpets.

She saw the blind boy sorting out the small

compartments in his trunk by the feel of each small article. Working on the tray that held different kinds of cartridges, he weighed and measured each one with his fingers.

"Can you tell a .44 from a .45 cartridge?" she asked.

"Talking about revolver shells?" he asked.

"Either way. Rifle or short gun, rim or center fire."

"Yes. This is a .45." He held out a pair of brass-cased cartridges for her to examine. "And this one is a .44."

She had to look at the stamping around the cap to be sure he was right.

"You can measure a hundredth of an inch by just the feel of the bullet?"

He nodded. "It takes a little practice. You going to shoot with Dog Kelly?"

"It's his idea," she said. "I'd just as soon stay out of it."

"He makes a living being crazy. Whenever he goes into a bank, they just hand over the money because they know he'll shoot everybody in sight if anything crosses him. Wind blows the wrong way, he'll shoot at it."

"I thought he was a miner," she said, puzzled.

"He robs banks and buries the money. Then he forgets where he buried it. And that makes him crazy mad. He's only dangerous when he's crazy mad."

"And that's most of the time," she said, nodding.

"No, you've never seen him with his eyes poppin' out and him foamin' at the mouth."

"What sets him off?" she asked.

"Folks call him Dog Kelly because he had this bulldog he loved like he was family. It was the only thing that could stand his smell. But Kelly went out looking for his money one time and got his directions turned around, and after a week of starvation, he ate the bulldog raw, nose to butt hole. . . . He ain't been right since."

"Thanks for telling me." She smiled.

The boy shook his head in solemn warning. "Whatever you do, don't ever call him Dog Kelly to his face."

Hardly had he delivered the warning than a boot came out of nowhere and sent the trunk over on its side, spilling out most of the small items.

"Whoops! I'm so clumsy!" Scars brayed, walking on across the street. "I must be blind!"

As the boy righted the chest and knelt down to repack the trays, she bent beside him to help out.

"Leave me alone!" the boy said sharply.

She stood and moved back, surprised at his anger.

"I don't help nobody and nobody helps me. Understand?" he burst out.

As he deftly sorted out his wares, he said, "I ain't mad. It's just that sooner or later you'll get killed, same as everybody in this town, so it's best not to get too close to people."

"I'm not going to get killed," she said levelly, "but you can't be sure until the Jamboree's over, can you?"

"You don't need a Jamboree to get killed here."

The boy shook his head. "They tell me the grave-yard's running out of room."

As gunmen came out of the saloon and people began lining the street, she looked up at the clock and saw that it was five minutes of two.

"Who's shooting?" she asked the boy.

"Spotted Horse and Carlos Montoya," the blind boy said. "Spotted Horse is favored eight to five."

Moving out of the way, she took a vantage point at the end of the porch and watched as the Mexican came out of the saloon and took his place in the middle of the street.

"Where is everybody?" he complained to Horace, frowning at the sparse audience.

"It's hot," Horace said. "Folks are takin' their siestas."

"Puta madre," Montoya snapped. "I'm not going to fight with nobody watching."

"Shut up!" came the whiplike command of John Herod striding down the boardwalk. Behind him, Cort was being half dragged along by two of Herod's councillors while the third one eyed the street and roofs carefully.

"That Indian *cabrón*, he ain't even here!" Montoya protested.

"If he isn't here when the clock sounds, he'll be eliminated," Herod said, and took his seat on the bench in front of the firehouse, with Cort being shoved to the ground at his feet.

Herod's wearing him down, she thought, watching

the tall preacher's head nod forward, then snap back, fighting to keep alert. It's his plan. Keep him awake, beat him, humiliate him, and after a while he'll revert back to the killer Herod wants.

The clock read one minute to two, and Horace yelled, "Gentlemen, take your positions and prepare to fire."

From out of nowhere the huge Indian materialized. Belted around his black suit coat was a beaded buckskin gun belt that held an old Starr Army .44.

The clockworks cranked, and as the chime sounded, Montoya drew quickly and fired five times to Spotted Horse's once. Both men, driven backward, fell to the ground. Montoya, with a bullet in his chest, dug his spurs into the dirt, belched loudly and rolled over on his side. Doc Wallace shambled into the street, looked down at the dead Mexican, then moved on to Spotted Horse, coughing and holding his chest with his left hand. Yet by the time Doc arrived, he climbed slowly to his feet and, holstering his gun, moved through the hushed crowd to the saloon steps. His face was dark and impassive as he said to Horace, "Spotted Horse have good medicine."

Two hours later big-hatted Virgil Sparks faced Scars, and the crowd came out in force. As the clock chimed four, Sparks tried to even the odds by drawing and diving flat into the street at the same time, but Scars's .44 was already in his hand. Before Sparks could get off a shot, Scars shot him through the crown of the big hat and punched a hole down through Sparks's head.

Scars holstered his six-gun and whacked a hatch mark on his left arm with his Bowie knife. "That's twenty-two." He grinned as the photographer recorded the moment.

"Dumb sonofabitch," Herod said disgustedly as he watched Charlie Moonlight box up Sparks's hardly marked body. "You can't win this game playin' tricks."

Heading for the saloon, Herod jerked his head toward Cort and said to one of his councillors, "Bring goody-goo-goo boy along and make sure nobody gives him a piece of bread."

The crowd parted for them as they marched into the Old Bank, and she saw anger rising on Cort's face that wasn't there before.

Herod's winning, she thought. Herod always gets his own way.

And then she asked herself what difference did this bedraggled and whipped-down preacher make to her.

Something, she thought, otherwise she wouldn't be thinking about him all the time.

Following along, she stood beside Scars at the bar and looked up at the chalkboard. The posted odds were ten to one against her.

Horace's daughter, Katie, asked what she wanted, and she settled for a short beer.

"Well look what the ten-cent whorehouse turned

down." She heard Dog Kelly screech from behind her.

She turned to see Kelly glaring at her with his bulging red-rimmed eyes, a glass of brandy in his grimy hand, a newly lit cheroot poking out of the corner of his mouth. Kelly looked around at the men playing cards at the tables and saw they were laughing with him.

She looked at them. . . . Dred, Simp Dixon, Dick O'Toole, even Herod was smiling.

Shrugging, she chuckled and went along with the game.

"You know, I probably won't just kill her. I think I'll just shoot off one of her big tits and have it fried up for breakfast."

The cardplayers laughed louder, enjoying some relief from the violence in the street, and she joined in with them.

As the crowd waited for more of Kelly's humor, she asked, "Mr. Kelly, now that we're fried bosom friends and all, do you mind if I call you by your nickname?"

The entire saloon hushed, a chair leg scraped the floor as someone moved aside. Kelly's left eye twitched.

"I ain't got no nickname," Kelly said hoarsely.

Behind her, Horace scrubbed off their odds and changed them from ten to one to twenty to one.

"Scars told me you had a nickname," she said, frowning.

Scars frowned. "I didn't say nothin'."

She took the cigar from Kelly's blackened teeth and leaned closer to him. "It was something to do with your favorite meal. Sowbelly Kelly? Chili Bowl Kelly? Smelly Jelly Kelly . . . ?"

"I ain't got no nickname," Kelly roared, his whole body twitching now, his face turning from rose to purple.

She drew on the cigar and puffed smoke in his face.

"I remember now. . . ."

She started to hand the cigar back to Kelly but managed instead to drop it into his brandy glass.

"Dog Belly Kelly," she said plainly.

Kelly exploded in insane rage. Dropping the brandy glass, he reached back and swung a long haymaker at her face, giving her plenty of time to duck, and Kelly's fist smacked Scars in the mouth.

Scars instinctively lashed back, driving the smaller Kelly against the wall.

Crazed, Kelly rushed back at him, and half the people in the saloon tried to pull the two of them apart as she quietly went out the bat-wing doors into the fresh air.

In a corner of the saloon, young Katie served Herod a plate of fried chicken and a glass of water. "Anything else, Mr. Herod?"

Herod ignored her, and she turned politely to Cort, sitting across the table. "Something for you, mister?"

"Get out of here," Herod growled, eyeing her contemptuously.

"Yes, sir," she said hurriedly and backed away.

Taking a bite out of a drumstick, Herod tossed the remainder in front of Cort and said, "Eat."

Cort ignored the mangled chicken leg and Herod's command.

Three shots sounded from the street, and in a moment Horace entered the saloon and ran a line through the name of Red Buckley on the blackboard.

Looking at his tin watch, he announced to the idling customers, "Next fight is Cort against Flat Nose. Right now there's no odds because nobody knows what this Cort jasper can do. Or if he could, will he?"

"He will," Herod said, tossing a clean wishbone aside and standing. "And I'll bet a hundred dollars to one he drops Flat Nose with one shot." Turning to Cort, Herod said, "It's about time."

Two councillors in their distinctive tan dusters jerked Cort to his feet, and Herod leaned his big shoulders forward. "I'm going to give you a gun and you're going to fight."

"Can't you get it through your head, I'm not the same man I used to be," Cort said strongly.

"We'll see." Herod walked out the bat-wing doors with Cort hobbling along under escort.

Herod walked catty-cornered across to the Kid's gun shop, and Ratsy met Cort and his escort outside with the keys to Cort's manacles.

"Allow me, gents." Ratsy showed his small protruding teeth in a smile and unlocked the handcuffs and leg irons.

"Now," Ratsy said, nodding to Cort, "just follow the leader."

As Cort staggered forward trying to get the circulation back in his hands and legs, Ratsy kicked him hard, sending him stumbling into the dust.

From across the street she saw Cort's face harden in disbelief, and anger suffuse his planed-down features, but he quickly regained control and got to his feet.

"Show me the other cheek," Ratsy laughed, "and I'll kick you the extra mile."

Again as Cort started for the steps of the gun shop, Ratsy kicked him, slamming him into the stone steps.

Grabbing the battered man by the collar, Ratsy boosted him on up the steps, and at the doorway turned to the crowd and said with a bitter chuckle, "Here endeth the first lesson."

Grabbing Cort by the shoulder, he threw him head first against the door, springing it open and sending Cort inside on hands and knees.

Cort shook his head, trying to gain a few seconds to clear his mind, and as Ratsy swaggered through the open door, Cort suddenly kicked the door back into Ratsy's face, sending the smaller man back down the steps.

Disturbed by the noise, Herod turned, looked over at Cort and said with a taunting smile, "I'm shocked," then turning to the smiling Kid, added, "His serene Reverence needs a gun."

"If you're buying, I'll bring out the cheapies." The Kid held his mocking smile.

"Your mouth gets faster every day. It's a pity your hands are so slow."

"My hands ain't slow," the Kid said, his grin turning to a grim, hateful slash.

"Put your hands on the table, Kid," Herod said, making up his own smile, taking the play away from the Kid.

The Kid watched the older man carefully, trying to fathom what trick he had in mind.

"Go on, Kid, I'd break your head instead of your hand if I meant to hurt you. Put it on the table."

Carefully the Kid spread his hands on the table and Herod laid his own next to it.

"See?" Herod said quietly, "yours are over-muscled, big, stiff joints, even callused. You've got hands like a farmer and I've got hands like a gunman. Believe me, there's a difference."

Jerking his hand away, the Kid said hatefully, "I ain't got farmer's hands."

Herod ignored the Kid's murderous expression, which was what he wanted in the first place, and winked at Cort.

"Now Cort and me, we're killers. Real number-one pure quill killers. But you, boy, you're from a different stock. . . . Now, my man here needs a gun."

The Kid, ready to explode, opened a glass case and

brought out three premium hand guns, each inlaid elegantly and with carved grips of pearl and ivory.

The Kid handled them lovingly, placing them gently on a piece of black velvet on top of the case.

"This one," the Kid said with renewed authority, "is an eagle-bill Smith & Wesson Schofield .45 with the seal of Mexico inlaid on the grip. Only thirty ever made because the handwork cost so much. This one is a rechambered Remington .44, more accurate even than a Colt. I took the walnut grips off and replaced them with solid turquoise, used on thirty-six—no, thirty-five successful bank robberies by its late owner. And here's the best helper a man can have, the Colt Peacemaker. Just a bread and butter piece, still, Jesse James and I think it's the best handgun in the world. I've cut away the trigger guard and filed down the sear, saves time when you need it, but don't draw it when you're drunk or you'll amputate your feet."

Cort stared at the gun like a hungry man looking at a menu, or like a reformed drunk gazing at an open bottle of cognac.

"I've turned down a hundred and twenty dollars for the Colt," the Kid said. "Go ahead, feel the balance."

Cort stared at the gun and thought it wouldn't hurt to just heft it, see how it felt.

Picking up the Colt, he twirled the cylinder to see that it wasn't loaded, then hefted it in both hands, tossed it almost playfully into the air, caught it with his left hand, aimed and dry-fired. Laying the barrel alongside his head, he drew the pistol slowly down by his ear as if listening to its inner spirit.

"You got a hundred and twenty-five dollars, Reverend?" Herod murmured.

"I have no money," Cort said quietly. "Providence provides what little I need."

Flushed with anger, Herod grabbed the Colt out of Cort's hands, and, gaining control, forced a sorrowful note into his voice. "Well then—I guess we're just wasting the farmer boy's time."

"Easy there, Mr. Mayor," the Kid said coldly, "I sell guns but I don't eat shit."

Herod smiled broadly and said apologetically, "I beg your pardon. I killed a farmer once because he was looking crossways at your mother."

"I heard," the Kid said flatly.

"I'll tell you what—" Herod said benignly, "I'll be a good Samaritan. I'll stand in for Providence and buy this poor pastor a weapon. An inexpensive piece, if you please."

The Kid put back his three best revolvers and brought out a plain Civilian Model Single Action Colt .44 with black rubber grips and laid it in front of Cort.

"Cost sixteen new," the Kid said. "You can have it for ten."

"Inexpensive," Herod rasped. "I mean the cheapest, most worthless piece of iron you've got in the store!"

The Kid glared angrily at Herod, then rummaged through an old ammunition box full of salvaged parts and brought out a converted 1851 Confederate Navy, barrel rusted, brass frame corroded, its broken grips wound with wire, and the front sight filed off.

Slamming it on the counter, the Kid said curtly, "Five dollars."

"Sold," Herod said, laying out five cartwheels as the Kid commenced loading the old six-gun from a new box of cartridges.

"Hold up there," Herod said. "With Providence guiding his hand, the preacher only needs one cartridge. One only."

The door opened and Ratsy poked his head in. Holding his hand over his damaged nose, he said, "Oh, Mr. Herod . . . it's time."

The Kid looked at Cort apologetically and said, "I don't cheat on guns. This one will shoot straight or I wouldn't sell it."

Herod dug out an old gun belt and holster from a box half full of leather scraps and, flipping it around Cort's waist, drew it through the buckle and jerked it a notch too tight.

"I won't draw," Cort said softly. "I won't fight. I won't do anything you want."

"You just think so, Cort," Herod said with assurance. "I know you too well. When it comes down to kill or be killed, you'll pull the trigger, and what's more, you'll like it."

Herod nodded to Ratsy, who grabbed Cort by the shoulders and pushed him out the door and on down into the street, not bullying now that Cort wore the gun.

She was waiting alongside the shoeshine stand when she saw the battered old six-gun on Cort's hip and guessed what had happened.

The street was lined with gunmen and townsfolk anxious to see Flat Nose down the preacher. Insults and jeers greeted Cort as he stood in the street. Someone shied a wet horse bun at him that bounced off his neck. Staring at the ground, he prayed quietly for the strength to stay true to his faith.

Looking up, he saw her standing by the blind boy, shook his head, shrugged.

Despairing, she understood that he would not defend himself and would be meat for Charlie Moonlight in a few minutes.

"Do it!" she screamed at him, but her voice was drowned out by Flat Nose's supporters, who were yelling, "Kill that sanctified sonofabitch!" "Give the bastard a halo!" "Don't shoot for his nuts, he ain't got any," one drunken wag yelled.

Flat Nose's kids came running at Cort, screaming insults and taunting him with obscene epithets. "Dead dead dead!" they screamed and threw manure from the street at him until Flat Nose stepped out into the far end of the street and yelled, "Get out of my way, you little shits!"

A whiskey bottle in his left hand, Flat Nose waved

at the crowd and listened to their encouragement. "Kill him slow, give us a show!" "Break his knees first, then work on up!" "Come on, Flat Nose, show us the color of his blood!"

Beside her the blind boy nervously worked one of his cartridges through his fingers as he cocked his head, listening.

"He won't," the blind boy said into the building tension, "and I bet a dollar he would."

Grinding out each minute, the clock, plainly begging for a shot of oil, crunched out another minute and the larger hand stood close to five.

The crowd quieted down.

Flat Nose took his stance. Left foot forward, right hand extended, sideways, a ferocious scowl which he thought the crowd would enjoy twisting his face.

Cort waited, his shoulders diffident, his eyes on the street but his mind in another sphere as he asked for support for his resolve.

She looked at the rooftops and saw the three sharpshooters in their tan dusters, their carbines slanted down, not at Flat Nose, because they knew he would play the game, but at Cort, who, if he didn't fight and Flat Nose somehow managed to miss, would be executed on the spot.

Damn him, she thought. She'd seen something decent and manly in him when they'd first brought him in, and in saving his life she'd lost track of her goal, and because of that diversion in her plans, she'd lost her courage when she'd had her chance to kill Herod. Now he was going to throw it all away while that demonic gila monster leaned back on his private bench and watched him die.

"The hell with it," she muttered to herself.

"You mean he ain't worth the powder to blow him to hell?" the blind boy asked.

"No, I'm just thinking he's the only man in town who doesn't care about living." She stared down at the boardwalk, not wanting to watch the slaughter.

The clock rumbled and commenced its chime.

Flat Nose's hand whipped to his side, jerked the revolver free of its holster and fired a quick snap shot that missed.

Settling down, he grinned and aimed, when BLAM! his arm jerked sidewise, his Colt flying off to the ground. The burning ache of the ragged wound in his upper arm made him want to throw up.

Sinking to his knees from surprise and shock, Flat Nose cried out, "He cheated! He shot me!"

Silence took over the street as Flat Nose wept from the pain and Doc Wallace shambled out with his black bag, looked at the arm and muttered, "You'll live if you don't get blood poison."

"Clean it up, Doc, please," Flat Nose sobbed.

Doc Wallace opened his bag, put Flat Nose's elbow on his knee and, after ripping off the shirt sleeve, poured a measure of iodine into the wound.

"Oh God Jesus Christ sonofabitch!" Flat Nose screamed as the iodine cauterized the raw flesh and he fainted dead away.

"Take him home," Doc Wallace growled at the five dumbstruck kids staring at their father lying in the street.

"Ain't you goin' to bandage it?" the oldest boy stammered.

"No point in it," the doctor said, "it'll heal of itself. If the flies get at it, all the better."

"You want him to lose his shootin' arm, don't you!" the next oldest snarled at the old doctor.

"To tell the truth, I don't give a damn," the old doctor muttered, and shuffled off toward his office.

Cort remained standing in the street, disgusted with himself. He'd stood for the first shot, but his resolve had broken when he'd seen Flat Nose taking deliberate aim at him. The rest had been automatic.

Herod strolled out to him and smiled. "Felt natural, didn't it, like you were born to it. You've still got the touch. I guess it's something like swimming— once you learn it, you never forget it."

"I'm sick of myself," Cort said, "and sick of your whole Jamboree. Turn me loose, please."

"You'll go free when the Jamboree is over, Cort," Herod said in a reasonable tone of voice. "Don't be such a sour apple. Let's have some fun."

"I tell you, Herod, I'm done with this life. You tolled me into it when I was a fool kid, but I quit it when I knew better, and I mean to stay quit."

"You don't know anything better'n the gun, Reverend. Why not relax and enjoy it?"

"I guess when it finally gets down to it, you want to justify your existence by shooting me," Cort said.

"But listen, John, I understand all that, I understand your feeling that killing keeps you strong, and I forgive you for it."

"You sonofabitch," Herod roared, truly provoked this time. "You don't ever talk about forgiving to me. I've been patient with you, welcoming you back to the fold, and ready to kill the fatted calf for you, but don't you ever talk about forgiveness to me!"

"It's the way I feel," Cort said simply.

"Maybe it'd be tolerable if I could forgive them that laid down and enforced their rules on me," Herod said more deliberately, "but they're dead, and Cort, my dear, when you change, it is you who will beg for forgiveness."

6

SHE SAW RATSY GRAB THE GUN FROM HIM AND CLAMP the manacles on Cort's wrists, then slam his fist into his lower back.

"That's for bustin' my nose!" Ratsy hissed, shoving him toward the boardwalk.

As he came closer, she tried to catch his eyes, but he kept his head down, humbled.

"You're pretty fast. I hope I don't have to fight you," she said quietly.

He glanced up at her then, hangdog sick of himself.

"Being here is your choice. I don't have any choice at all," he muttered.

She saw the brooding pain in his eyes, and looking down, she saw blood serum oozing from his wrists where the manacles had chafed through the skin.

"He made you do it. You're way outnumbered."

"I'm the only one that pulled the trigger. Thank God I didn't kill him," Cort said, not accepting her commiseration.

"This is no place for a preacher." She wondered why he would not look her squarely in the eye.

That he was a prisoner in chains, helpless, worse off even than a slave in bondage, was obvious, but what had he done that humbled him so? What terrible crisis had bonded him with Herod, a nexus neither one of them could absolve or pardon, forgive or forget.

"I wasn't always a preacher," he murmured, shaking his head, not looking at her, but knowing the question in her mind. "I'm trying to change, but—"

"Killin' is like a good cigar. Once you get a taste for it, the more the better." From behind them came Herod's rich, muddy drawl.

"I—" Cort started to protest, but was overridden by Herod's more powerful assurance.

"Cort was an outlaw just like the rest of us, only twice as bad. We rode side by side but he worked extra hard. He'd even stay up nights figuring a plan to take over some town and plunder the guts out of it."

She turned and saw the smile on Herod's broad mouth, but she saw nothing but fire-limned darkness in his eyes. She looked back at the abject Cort and an expression of hostile reprehension crossed her face.

"That's all changed now," Herod continued jovially. "He's a man of peace. Wouldn't hurt a fly.

Probably kisses babies. All that blood on his hands washed away by the blood of the lamb. I never could figure that out. Now he's trying to look like a milksoppin' son of God, but lady, deep down, he's no different than me."

Herod laughed as he turned away, and she looked at Cort disgustedly. "I should have let him hang you."

Staring at his feet, Cort had nothing to say, no defense or excuse or pleas for understanding. He stood as a man with a tortured soul haunted by his past and fearful of his own self-betrayal.

She felt no pity—rather she wanted to be clear of his wretched mien, his helpless spirit dodging back and forth in its cage, seeking a way out to glory and peace, yet still gripped by the bloodlust of mortal man.

Following along after John Herod, she saw him stroll across the street toward a group of lesser outlaws and townsfolk grouped around Ace Hanlon, who was signing autographs on scraps of paper with a pen dipped in a vial of red ink.

"I'll sign anything but counterfeit bank drafts." Hanlon smiled as a timid-faced youngster extended a new cream-colored holster which, with Ace Hanlon's signature on it, might be blessed with good luck.

"Thank you very much, Mr. Hanlon," the youth said gratefully. "I'm much obliged to you, and I sure hope you win the big money."

"My pleasure, son," Ace Hanlon said grandly, hardly listening as someone pushed a notebook at him, "and thank you for your good wishes."

As Hanlon wrote his name and drew an ace of spades in red ink in the notebook, Herod asked conversationally, "Mr. Hanlon, I've always wanted to ask you about Indian Wells. Did that fight really happen the way folks say?"

"Sure did." Ace Hanlon looked up as he handed the notebook back to an awestruck little girl.

"And you gunned down four top shooters, like one-two-three-four?" Herod smiled wickedly.

The autograph seekers faded away under the clashing voices.

Charlie Moonlight quit throwing clean sand from a wheelbarrow over the gouts of blood in the street and returned to his carpentry shop.

The street stood empty and quiet.

"Two with my left hand," Ace Hanlon said, eyeing Herod carefully and backing away to gain more room. "Two with my right. You see, I'm just as good either way."

She studied their subtle footwork and how their hands moved, the way their bodies shifted, engaging in an invisible and tentative attack and counterattack, practicing thrusting and feinting in anticipation of the explosive volley soon to come.

She saw Herod savoring the moment, joy glinting in the fire pits of his eyes, scorn tipping his wide mouth.

"Why, you must be the fastest gun in the territory, Mr. Hanlon." He glanced up at the clock showing a minute to six. "Either that or the biggest liar."

"Pity you weren't there, I'd have made it five." Ace Hanlon moved his left boot back so that his right side turned toward Herod.

Calmly, Herod took his time slipping a black silk glove over his right hand. Tugging it up tight, he smoothed out the small wrinkles around his fingers and, looking off at Hanlon, said, "But I was there. I don't know where you were, but I was the man who shot the four Terence brothers, one-two-three-four, and I just doubt a lying tinhorn chickenshit card-sharp like you was even in the state."

Hanlon paled as the clock rumbled and clanged the hour, and his hand stabbed down, palmed his .44, lifted it free.

She saw Herod's knees bend slightly, but the rest was a blur of fluid motion nearly invisible to the naked eye.

Ace Hanlon's right hand exploded into a mangled club of jagged white bones and torn tendons, his nickel-plated .44 careening free.

In agony, he clutched the destroyed hand in his left hand, hunching his shoulder against the pain.

As Herod holstered his golden six-shooter, he said breezily, "Let's try the other hand, Ace. Show everybody how fast that left can draw and fire."

She saw Hanlon's sick white face, saw his whole body quake in fear, saw his eyes seek some avenue of escape, saw hopelessness rise in his face, and saw

Herod waiting as patiently as Old Man River, smiling.

"You can do it, Ace. A hard-assed two-gun man like you wouldn't think about running off like a yellow-gutted coyote, he'd just stand up and fight like a real man."

Ace Hanlon nodded to himself. Carefully, he wiped the blood off his left hand on the inner thigh of his pants leg, the hand moving closer to the pearl-handled .44.

She wondered if Herod could see the advantage Hanlon was creating for himself, when suddenly Hanlon's good hand came up with the Colt and he sidestepped to the left.

Instantly, out of the same supernatural blur of motion, Herod's gun bloomed and what was left of Hanlon's left hand poked vainly as if the cold gun were still in it, as if the absent trigger finger was snapping off shots, their recoil jerking the wrist.

Hanlon stared at the welter of meat and bone that had once been so quick with the cards and groaned like a gut-shot bull. A wet stain spread down the inside of his fawn-colored trouser legs and leaked to the ground.

"Say good riddance to Ace Hanlon, Pacifier of El Paso, Terror of Tucson, Poor Puke of Redemption," Herod announced grandly, and fired again. This time the bullet tore off Hanlon's slouch hat.

Transfixed, Hanlon stupidly gaped at Herod.

"Just a willy wet-leg after all," Herod added coldly, shaking his head, and then, in a rush of annoyed disgust, he tipped the golden gun up again and fired.

The mercy shot dotted Hanlon's forehead and snapped his head back, slamming him down to the street where his dead body pitched and trembled in nervous spasms.

The crowd, only a moment before petrified by the seething gore and Herod's ruthless domination, broke into scattered applause as Herod slowly stripped off the black glove. Contemptuously, he glanced at the crowd, daring any one of them to object or protest, but as he scanned the faces, the applause grew, the whole town cheering its champion.

She was unmoved, and she thought the people were not cheering out of respect, to honor their hero, but to avoid his fearful wrath.

Gazing at the big-shouldered, contemptuous man, she felt her own tremor of fear, because the demon she must destroy looked to be immortal. Better to hunt a grizzly bear with a switch than face that man with a gun.

She felt an oppressive humidity, saw the dark clouds overhead turning into thunderheads, heard the snarl of the wind gusting up the street.

"What are you shaking for?" the blind boy beside her asked. "You want a half pint of Napoleon?"

"I feel cold," she lied, and took the small bottle of cognac from his hand, jerked the stopper and tilted the bottle to her lips.

As John Herod strode up the street toward his

mansion without bothering to acknowledge the applause, the crowd edged out toward the body of Ace Hanlon.

Flat Nose's kids poked at it with sticks, and suddenly Dog Kelly grabbed at the white calfskin boots, pulling them off the dead man's feet and giving the signal to the others to plunder the corpse.

Eugene Dred elbowed his way through and grabbed the tie pin made of black jet in the shape of the ace of spades and outlined by bloodred rubies.

In no time the body was stripped down to soiled and bloody underwear, and as Charles Moonlight arrived with his black cart, the mutilated and disfigured carcass was hoisted aboard like a fresh side of beef.

Watching the cart head off toward the graveyard, she thought of herself, her own body blasted to dead meat, stripped and whittled at, then carried on that black dray down the trail.

In the distance she saw the glow of lightning. From the mountains came the low rumble of thunder.

Her face ashen, her fingers balled up into fists to hide the trembling, she strode quickly through the saloon and climbed the stairs to her room.

She thought the thunder was coming closer, and pulling down the shade, she leaned weakly against the door, wondering how she could ever avenge the violent and degrading death of her father. That she must, was certain. The how was not so certain. For true revenge the killer must die but the avenger must live. Otherwise it made no sense.

John Herod must die and know why, and she must somehow survive.

O dear God, she whimpered as thunder rolled down the distant mountains and across the plain.

Sitting back on the bed, she hugged herself as the thunder tolled across like hundreds of horses' hooves beating their way toward the town, and she remembered the green clover blooming in the street . . . heard the child's voice . . .

"Jesus loves me
This I know,
For the Bible tells me so . . ."

. . . the claws of the bearded man dragging her inside a doorway . . . then peeking out. . . .

Again a clap of thunder that sounded like a ripping of pistol shots. She shuddered and winced, and then understood it was hammering on the door and young Katie's voice breaking through her nightmare. "Lady! Lady, they're callin' for you. It's time!"

Not waiting, Katie pushed open the door, and seeing her lying disheveled on the bed, said excitedly, "It's coming up on seven. They want you down there. . . ."

She stared at the girl, fitting the day's pieces back together.

"You all right? Are you really goin' to face a man? What if you're slow? What if you miss?" Katie yattered on.

"You better start using your noodle, girl, or you'll

end up worse'n dog meat," she said irritably, rising and pouring water from the pitcher into the ewer.

"I don't get it, lady," Katie said, puzzled.

"That's the problem, girl. You don't know."

"What don't I know?"

"Living here like you do, you don't know women shouldn't get fucked for a quarter," she said, scrubbing life into her somber face.

"What's that got to do with shooting with Dog Kelly?" Katie asked, feeling threatened and frightened. "What if you get killed?"

"Then I guess I won't be around to answer any more of your dumb questions," she said, buckling on her gun belt.

As Katie started out the door, she had a second thought and turned. "Lady—"

"What now!" she demanded angrily.

"You can do it," Katie said, smiling, and closed the door behind her.

Before leaving the room, she checked the loads in her .44, adding a sixth cartridge to the chamber she usually left empty for the sake of safety.

Crazy, she thought. If you don't kill him with your first shot, he'll have you beat. Still, suppose it came to where she'd used up five shots, then she'd be damned glad she had the extra.

Forcing herself to go slow, she went down the stairs and out into the street. The clock said two minutes to seven, and she saw that the storm clouds had brought on dusk earlier than usual.

She saw the crowd waver in her vision. Men

drinking, townsfolk hesitant but lured by a deep-seated blood carnality to watch a woman die in battle. She saw the blind boy looking vainly about, working a brass-cased cartridge around through his fingers nervously.

She saw Dog Kelly standing in the street, still livid with rage, and as she passed by Cort in chains, she stared straight ahead, ignoring him.

"You're goin' to die the hard way!" Dog Kelly squalled. "I'm goin' to blow you to doll rags and then I'm gonna scalp you low!"

She heard Cort whisper, "There's a click before the strike."

"What?" she asked, startled.

"Listen to the clock."

Stepping into the street, she saw Horace watching the clock.

"Get on with it!" someone yelled.

Horace looked relieved that she was there and ready, and announced, "Ladies and gentlemen! On my left is that famous nemesis of banks, Mr. Kelly! And on my right is the mysterious beauty, Miss . . . Smith?" Horace looked at her hopefully, wanting a name.

"Leave off the Miss," she said shortly. "Just call me Death."

"Ah . . . the mysterious beauty . . . Death!" Horace cried out fearfully. "It's the last fight of the day. Everybody enjoy yourselves, and may the best shooter win!"

"Get out of my way," she said curtly, and as the

bartender scuttled off the street, she watched Dog Kelly settle into position, holding his hands level with his chest and loosening them up.

"I hate to kill what's maybe a good piece of ass. . . ." He grinned.

"Yum, yum, bulldog!" she taunted him, and saw his hands lock up into iron vises.

She wiped her sweating hand on her thigh and waited in the somber, tomblike silence for the clock to clear its throat.

She heard the click that Dog Kelly had been confidently waiting for and they drew almost simultaneously. Hands blurring gripping pulling leveling firing.

Dog Kelly's shot went screaming over the crowd into the storm clouds. Bucked backward by her soft lead bullet, Kelly fell squirming to the ground. Grabbing at his left shoulder, he blatted like an anxious sheep, "Oh God! Oh shit! Oh Sweet Jesus! Oh damn it all, I'm bleeding. Somebody help, I'm sure to bleed to death . . . ! Don't just stand there watching. . . ."

Doc Wallace rambled over to him, tore the shirt free and examined the wound.

"You'll live, but you won't be using that arm much anymore, Lefty," Doc Wallace said, applying a thick cotton compress to the wound.

She felt drained of energy, but she stood tall and slowly holstered the Colt, trying to hide the small tremble in her hand. Dog Kelly's friends hollered their hateful diatribes at her, but the townspeople shyly applauded, watching out of the corners of their eyes in case someone with a gun disapproved.

As she started for the boardwalk, Horace rushed out on the street and announced, "The Lady . . . Lady Death is the winner. Everybody be here at noon tomorrow for the second eliminations round!"

As she left the street, the mob hooted and booed and brayed and headed back into the saloon.

She saw John Herod staring at her, and when he caught her eye, he gave her a nod of approval, while Cort, like a chained slave beside him, looked down at his boots.

She noticed Eugene Dred sitting on the porch of the saloon and Katie standing at his shoulder.

Shyly, Katie stepped forward and said to her, "Gosh, Lady . . . I think you're just great!"

"Grow up, kid," she said coldly. "Get smart, or get out of this town."

Knowing that advice to pretty little fillies was generally wasted, she rebuked herself for trying to set this kid straight, and entering the saloon, she looked for a table. She felt weary enough to just sit on the floor, lean back against the wall and watch the world go by, but she could not show any weakness in front of the respectful crowd.

Respect, she thought bitterly. How can anybody respect violence, whether it comes from a gun or club or fist?

Nobody respected the whores that sweated and degraded themselves like mules for Eugene Dred, who did nothing but preen his finery and give them a clout if they failed to produce the money. What was the difference? she wondered. He was a man. He carried a gun and wasn't afraid to use it to protect his interests, and yet he'd stand by any bully who wanted to pee in a woman's face or stick his fist up her cunt . . .

. . . And like a good, loyal dog seeking a pat on the head from her master, the poor stupid whore would hand over the money before it was even done.

Respect! Jesus Christ, people only respected power, and who had the most power of anybody? Mr. John Herod, sadist-killer.

Passing close to the bar, she watched as the giant Indian Spotted Horse faced Horace across the bar and yelled, "I can not be killed!"

The packed crowd quieted down a little, waiting for more.

Slinging away his coat and ripping his striped shirt off, Spotted Horse exposed his scar-dimpled torso.

"Look at that," he said, tapping the scars. "I've taken bullets in my arms and legs, two in my back, goddamn the sonsabitches to hell! One through my jaw, three through the lungs, and one through the heart! Then that one went through here today," he said, touching an inflamed point just below his bottom rib. "It ain't come out yet. Great Spirit sticks white man's bullets up white man's ass."

Getting the drift of his brag, believable or unbelievable, she found it uninteresting and moved over to an empty table.

Dully, she tried to gather up her forces of energy.

The day wasn't over. The Jamboree was not over. Herod was not dead.

Suddenly four glasses filled with liquid amber came to rest on the table, and she looked up to see the Kid on her right and Sergeant Quanson on her left, both men looking down at her possessively.

"Sorry, gents," she said, "I'm drinking rut beer tonight."

"Rut as in R-U-T?" The Kid grinned.

"No, rut as in no thanks."

Each man had his left hand on the single chair, and Sergeant Quanson said, "You've got your hand on my chair, sonny."

"I was here first, old-timer." The Kid looked hard at the black gunman. "Just what the hell is that piece of mineral growing out of your leg?"

"You talkin' about the Quanson Swivel?" Sergeant Quanson asked easily, turning so the Kid could see it better.

Instead of a standard gun belt and holster, the apparatus consisted only of a slotted metal strip riveted to the belt, and a Peacemaker with a stud welded to the steel strap over the cylinder—the first except for the early Root models—a stud that slid into the slot and rotated and trained without needing to be drawn clear of a holster.

"I made it and I practice enough. It beats anything in a quick-draw contest. I'm here to prove it."

"You better go practice some more, old-timer." The Kid grinned. "That thing'd be plumb worthless against a back-shooter."

"The contest is face-to-face," Quanson said, flicking the hammer and sending the Peacemaker into a whirling orbit that ended with the ivory grips in balance at the top, close to his big hand.

"I'm not a back-shooter, whatever else I am." The Kid held his smile. "It's just that this lady and me have shared——"

"Shared what?" came the baby-talk voice of Mattie Silk.

The Kid hunched his shoulders and turned to see the small, big-busted blond girl looking up at him.

"Shared stories," the Kid said. "How somebody fell off a cloud, how somebody else kept a warm bed on a stack of dynamite . . ."

"The Kid and me are going to be wedded soon. Ain't we?" she demanded of the Kid.

"That's what you're always tellin' me," the Kid said, irritated and embarrassed.

She smiled, feeling the pieces of herself coming together again, stronger than before.

"He's goin' to be the new mayor with a bunch of councillors, and we might just start up a gun factory here to give the people jobs, and we're goin' to find out where all the money is and who do we have to shoot to get it. . . ."

"Hush now," the Kid said, quailing. "You're talkin' too much!"

"Ain't that what you said, honey?" Mattie Silk looked at the Kid, puzzled.

"That's just talk. You know—dreams. It ain't like it was all for real."

"You mean sweet-talkin'?" Mattie Silk caressed his shoulder. "I understand that. . . ."

"There ain't much to talk about around here, you know. . . ." he said, trying to explain to the lady called Death.

In all the shouting-crazed drunken babble, she leaned forward to hear better, and saw the back of John Herod standing at the bar.

". . . and, well maybe it's a little soon to announce it, but just for your private information," Mattie Silk continued, like it was critically important, "we're gonna have the biggest wedding this town ever saw since Mr. Herod came to town! And what's more, that's the day I'll tell Mr. Eugene Dred that he can go find himself another workin' girl, and he can stuff this job right up his rosy red ass. . . ."

"Don't be in too big a hurry. Maybe sometime Mr. Eugene Dred might look like the best friend a sporting girl ever had," she said, wondering why she was waiting.

Herod held his head high, his carefully combed, graying hair shaped back over the nape of his neck.

One bullet through the base of the skull—that's all. As simple as pointing your finger and saying bang. She had made the same shot at a fast-moving target a thousand times. She'd blistered her hands and worked an ache in her shoulder practicing that shot so she could make it with her eyes closed.

Forgotten were the three inconspicuous councillors in tan dusters watching the noisy, unruly crowd.

Kill him! she screamed at herself as Mattie Silk

yammered on and Sergeant Quanson simply waited, knowing when he was outdone. The Kid backed away, gradually blending in with the congestion, Mattie saying, "We'll have us a cake about as high as the room can take, and I've already got the brides-maids picked . . ."

The back of his head, the curve of the gray-touched hair at the nape of his neck welcomed her like a beacon, signaling here is the brain just behind the shiny hair and a little shell of bone. . . . Perforate it—just crease it, blow it to pieces, and you can begin again on something called the road of life.

". . . and we'll move into the big house and I'll be easy on the servants . . . I mean, we can have a drink together after hours, you know . . . I'm not too bossy. . . ."

And she thought, there's his head. The back of it. Okay. What the hell difference does it make, back or front? Blow it apart like a goddamned cantaloupe and start fresh.

She slowly drifted her hand to the walnut grips of her .44 and felt more steady, more safe. Gripping the .44, she stared at the back of the head of the man she meant to kill.

Suddenly Herod turned, a quizzical look on his face, as if he'd heard a tale on the wind, a premoni-tion, a sixth sense telling him he was half a second from death. Turning, frowning, looking, he saw the resolution in her eyes and stared back at her.

She looked away fearfully, in panicked confusion.

Suddenly, crouching beside her, the old doctor in

the long black coat, with stinking breath, spoke into her ear urgently.

"You. I've got to talk to you."

"No," she said wearily, already defeated by Herod's invincibility.

Unheeding, obsessed, Doc Wallace grabbed at her shoulder, but she was twice too strong for him. Rising quickly, she jerked away and walked up the stairs.

As she reached the landing she dared look down. She met Herod's eyes, suspicious, bored, experienced, offering not even a challenge, sending the only message he knew: "Cross my path and lose your life."

=== 7 ===

SHE REACHED THE TOP OF THE STAIRWELL AND STARTED down the hall when she saw Eugene Dred looking like a bird of paradise in his florid costume, with his left arm around young Katie's waist. Coming closer, she saw he was dangling Ace Hanlon's ruby and jet tie pin in front of Katie's delighted eyes, and holding her close, bent down to kiss her. Katie didn't pull back. When he released her, Katie looked scared and flattered.

Coming close, she said, "I wasted some good advice on you."

Katie looked shamefaced at the floor.

"What're you lookin' at?" Dred growled.

"A dirty old whoremonger and a dumb kid," she said bitterly.

"I'm going to give her a chance to become a lady of

133

leisure instead of everybody's servant." Dred smiled like a crocodile.

"You be sure to wash careful wherever he touches you," she said to the girl, who flicked her eyes at the jeweled tie pin, then scurried down the hall.

"Sometime soon I'm going to stick something up your ass, and if you're lucky, it'll be a bullet," Dred snarled, and pushed on past her.

As she turned to open the door, she found the folded card stuck in the doorjamb.

The message written in flowing script said simply: *Dinner tonight. John Herod.*

Inside the room, she fetched out her saddlebags from under the bed and brought out a parcel wrapped in brown paper and another smaller one in a clean flannel cloth.

"Well, look who's hiding here. . . ." she said aloud, ironically, yet with an air of haunted poignancy.

Unwrapping the parcel, she brought out a simple navy-blue velvet dress, pleated fully around the hips, trimmed with lace and a row of silver buttons running down the right side from the waist to the hem. With it was a pale blue cashmere stole to cover her shoulders. Lifting the stole in her fingers, she thought it would float away on the slightest breeze, so light and fine it was, perfect for the heat, though, and elegant enough for any lady from Chicago.

The other bundle proved to be a more deadly sort of accessory. From the flannel covering, she lifted a small .41 caliber derringer with a hook grip and a three-inch barrel. It fitted easily in the palm of her hand. After checking the heavy rimfire cartridge, she fitted the gun back into the suede-covered spring grip that could be strapped to her leg or wrist out of sight.

That ought to do it, she thought, feeling the old fire of vengeance rising in her. Recalling the man's massive and ineluctable power, she thought that once you knew it, you could get around it. There was no reason for fear even though he radiated that powerful force, because after all, it was only an etheric vibration—a charged atmosphere that could not stop a heavy bullet. Once you figured that out, you'd neutralize your fear and just shoot him down deader'n a fried mule.

Changing into the gown, she realized she had not brought proper shoes and that her short black riding boots would have to do.

That's where they'll look for the gun, she thought, and smiled.

Looking at herself in the cracked mirror, she shifted her hips so the pleated skirt flared out and settled back again and she could see no bulge of the hideout gambler's gun.

Tying her golden hair back in a ponytail, she looked once more in the looking glass, looked into her own blue eyes and thought: You're not afraid of him. He's just a mortal man. You blow out his heart, he's nothing.

Shaking her head, she smiled ruefully at herself and murmured, "At least you hope so."

Downstairs, she slipped out the front door of the

saloon unnoticed, and going to the blind boy's shoeshine stand, she settled in the chair and said to the boy, "Shine 'em up, please."

"Black?" the boy asked, feeling the soft leather boots.

"Black."

"You smell different," the boy said, applying the polish with his fingers, rubbing it into the calfskin. "Where are you going all dressed up?"

"Dinner at the big house."

"Can I ask why?" the blind boy asked, feeling for his flannel cloth.

"I'm curious," she said. "I want to find out how he can twist everybody in this town around his little finger."

"I figure it's something extra he's got, an extra brain charger, extra purple blood, maybe a double-sized heart that beats twice as fast as anybody else's."

She chuckled. "That's funny."

"I hope you find out," the boy said, popping the cloth expertly over the toe of her burnished boot. "I'd sure like to know, too."

"What'd you do with the rest of that cognac?" she asked as he finished and rolled up the cloth.

"Right here." He fetched the small bottle out of the trunk and handed it to her. "You need it?"

"Damn right!" She tilted the bottle to her lips and finished it off.

"You drink too much," the boy said. "It'll let you down sometime when you want to be pushed up."

"You're right," she said, standing and dropping a gold coin into his cup. "It's a poor prop, but right now I need all the help I can get."

As she walked down the boardwalk, the whistling, taunting young men of yesterday moved aside respectfully. None of them had risked their lives in the street, she thought. That's where the power comes from.

It's dangerous, she thought, feeling a pleasure deep down as they stood aside. A weak person could take a liking for that kind of a feeling.

Past the square she saw Cort chained to a hitching post and she wondered if Herod had deliberately locked him there for the night just to watch her come and go.

He looked closely at her dress, the stole settled lightly over her hair and shoulders, the polished boots.

"You didn't need to go to all that trouble for me," he said, his voice rusty and dry.

"I didn't."

"Last night the Kid, tonight Herod. Busy lady. Anybody in town know you're not hustling?" he asked.

"You," she said curtly.

"Likely a bighearted lady would do me a little favor," he said, looking at a glass of water that sat farther out in the street than he could reach.

"If you could just take a moment to move that glass over this way, it would be of some use to somebody."

Deliberately she moved the glass a couple inches closer to his outstretched fingers, but still not within reach.

"How's that?" she asked contemptuously.

"You sure look fetching in that blue dress. Matches your eyes." He smiled grimly.

"Shouldn't you be praying or gnawing on your wrists like a rabbit in a steel trap?"

"I'm praying most of the time, but not for myself. I don't count anymore."

"What are you praying for, then?" She frowned, not understanding.

"Lost souls. Yours, Herod's, Dred's . . . ." he murmured.

"You lump me in with them?"

"I'd say I'm more worried about your soul than any of the others. You're different somehow. You don't fit in."

"Better pray you can walk like a man someday," she said sharply.

"You shoot pretty good, lady, but not as good as some others in this town. If you catch the killing fever, you won't last," he said seriously.

"I'm doing all right."

"You don't have killers' eyes." He shook his head.

"And you're not much of a parson either. I don't see you walking on water, or drinking any, either."

She shoved the glass over with her boot, spilling half of it on the ground, then strode angrily on toward the big house.

Cort watched her straight back, saw the play of pleats around her thighs, and drank what was left in the glass.

She paused in front of the marble statue of Jesus welcoming the little children with his outstretched hands. She saw the carved, bland smile, the carefully trimmed beard, the dead white eyes, and looking up, she saw a neat sign hanging from the porch: HEROD HOUSE.

Her stomach turned over with revulsion that this stone Christ should welcome her to a perverted church stolen from its lily-livered Christers.

Before she could climb the wide steps, she was met by the three armed councillors in their tan duster uniforms.

"I'll have to pat you down for weapons," one of them said, his hatchet face devoid of expression.

"Don't get any ideas," she said as he quickly ran his hands down her hips and then concentrated on the inside of the boots.

"Clean," the guard said and stepped back. "Just don't forget we're always close by watching."

"All night?" She glared at him.

"We don't go inside Mr. Herod's private quarters," the guard said, stepping aside.

Looking up at the broad front veranda, she saw John Herod standing there, holding out a chilled glass of champagne for her.

"Come on up, please," he called out with a smile. "It's worth the climb."

Not hurrying, she went up the steps and wondered why the original builders of the church had put it so high off the ground.

"I'm pleased that you came," he said in his thick Mississippi drawl, putting the glass in her left hand, touching his lips to the back of the right hand.

"Your courtesy is overwhelming," she said, turning to look out over the town.

She understood it then. The elders had wanted the church to be seen and looked up to by the town. Herod had reversed their thinking. He not only wanted the town to look up to him, he wanted to look down at the town. His town.

"This is a beautiful vista, especially with all the lanterns in the street," she said politely.

"I could have had the old church torn down and built my house here in my own way, but the idea of keeping a temple as an entrance hall appealed to my sense of the irony," he said smoothly, as if he'd practiced the speech many times. "Herod's house, at heart, is the church of the Master."

"It doesn't bother you that some martyred spook might come up out of the cellar and grab you by the ankle some night?" She grinned.

He chuckled. "Hardly. The spooks fear me as much as the rest of the second-raters out there."

Going inside, she saw the rich Persian carpets, the oil paintings of angels and cherubs on the walls, small alabaster statues of maidens dancing in gossamer tunics.

"I'll bet you think we have nothing in common,"

he said as he showed her through the richly decorated rooms, "but we do. We're both winners."

"So far."

"How does it feel to survive the first day?"

"Same as yesterday," she said carefully, pretending to drink the champagne, preparing herself for the moment of attack.

"No," Herod said comfortably, "your eyes are shining. You've passed a test. You feel alive, really alive. . . ."

"I guess it doesn't excite me as much as it does you." She shook her head.

"Do you think I have this contest for fun? No, no—this town is full of scum that would kill you for your boots." He chuckled. "This way I get to face my enemies before they can get set to shoot me in the back. Plus, of course, it's always a pleasure to win."

She glanced up at him, hoping her hatred wouldn't show.

"Maybe someday your luck will run out," she murmured.

"I don't win because I'm lucky." He smiled smugly.

"Your maid is very pretty," she said, "but she never spoke one word all through dinner."

"I haven't cut her tongue out," Herod said comfortably, "but early on I told her that if she ever talked about me or my business, I would do it. She's properly trained."

"And an excellent cook, too," she said, finishing the last of the strawberry shortcake.

They sat at a large dining table covered by a glistening damask cloth cleared except for the wineglasses, a decanter half full of Gewurtztraminer, and the china dessert plates. The candlesticks were heavy Georgian silver, and the yellow candles themselves were made of scented beeswax.

A mahogany Chippendale sideboard was incongruously littered with a brass telescope, a Spencer carbine, a pair of gold-plated six-guns, and bundles of currency carelessly tossed onto the polished mahogany.

"I thought the pheasant was a little dry," he said. "I'll speak to her about it."

She sipped at the aromatic wine with her left hand while her right hand returned to her lap.

"Why did you come here tonight?" he asked quietly.

She shrugged. "You invited me."

"You could have turned me down."

She reached for the wine decanter with her left hand, meaning to refill his empty glass, but his hand was faster and, taking charge, filled her own goblet to the brim.

"I wanted to see what kind of a man you are," she answered smoothly.

"And what kind of a man am I?" he murmured, staring at her.

"The kind people hate."

He smiled. "I'm not trying to be popular. The

people in my town *need* me. I bring order into their lives, not law and order. Just order. My way, they don't have to worry about anything."

"What about hanging the preacher in the saloon?" she asked. "That seemed some disorderly to me."

Even as she spoke she knew it was time to try. Much longer and he'd ask her to go to bed with him, and she didn't want to get that close.

Casually she moved her right hand from her lap to a silver button at the side of her skirt, and lifting the wineglass with her left to hold his attention, she took a sip.

"He's not a preacher, he's a fake!" Herod said angrily, ignoring all but her eyes. "If a man's a killer, then that's what he is. There's no dishonor about it. But if that exact same man suddenly tells me it's not in his blood anymore, then he's the worst kind of a lying two-faced polecat."

"Why's he upset you so much?" she asked, slipping her right hand through the open placket and finding the eagle-bill butted derringer.

Overriding her placid question, he said strongly, "I find myself almost uncontrollably attracted to you." Simply, but intensely, he added, "I hope you don't mind my saying that."

In the heart of that intensity shimmered the power that fired out beams of enthralling lightning flashes.

Struggling for control, she said, "I'm surprised that a man like you doesn't have a woman. Unless . . ."

"No, not the maid," he snapped. "Don't demean

me. To answer your question, I was married to a very beautiful woman . . . For reasons of her own, she was unfaithful."

Slipping the gambler's gun out of its clip and holding herself steady, she asked, "Where is she now?"

"I don't wish to ruin a good dinner with the grim details."

She stared at him, the single shooter palmed in her hand.

Suddenly he added, "Why are you really here? You're not a gunfighter."

"Like I said, for the prize money," she replied, poker-faced, and brought the small gun up into her lap. She wondered if her face was sweating. She wondered if her eyelids were trembling.

She knew she must pull the hammer back, which would force out the bit of trigger called a stud, but which she would have called a clit, then she must aim it straight across under the table, press the clit and punch a hole through his belt buckle and out his backbone.

One bullet. One chance.

"I could give you that box of money and more," he said.

"I wouldn't feel like I'd earned it."

"Don't fool yourself, you'd damn well earn every penny of it," he said harshly, his eyes bulging, projecting the force that made her tremble, and as she fumbled with the little gun, trying to quietly cock it, it slipped loose, skittered off her dress and fell into her right boot top.

"You ever killed anyone?" he asked intensely, leaning forward, cracking her will.

"Sure," she said, valiantly trying to maintain her composure as she lifted her right leg and sought for the gun with her outstretched fingers. Suddenly, the image of Cort's outstretched fingers reaching for the glass of water filled her mind and she felt like crying out "I'm sorry!" because now she knew how it felt.

"Are you feeling all right?" he asked, frowning.

"Just a little cramp in my foot," she said, bringing the derringer back to her lap.

Casually, he took a long cheroot from a silver humidor and rolled it between his fingers.

She knew he'd caught something of her clumsiness, but she couldn't know how much he'd guessed.

"I doubt you've killed, and I doubt if you would," he said, eyeing her steadily. "You see, everything comes down to the basic: How far are you prepared to go?"

Cupping the .41 derringer in her right hand, she aimed it under the table and cocked back the hammer. Trying and failing to completely cover the metallic ker-CHUNK, she said, too loudly, "All the way."

Herod's eyes hardened to pinpoints of blazing light as his clenched right hand drifted to his lap.

"My father was a judge down in Mississippi," he said, twisting her thinking again off the straight and certain path. "He used to make my mother and I watch his prisoners hang. He never would let their feet be tied nor would he drop them far enough to break their necks. He liked to see them strangle slow while their legs flailed out crazily. . . ."

"Horrible!" she said sickly, unable to bring herself back to the single focused goal as she saw in her mind's eye her father slumped at the end of a rope while a strange child wept. . . .

"One day," Herod continued, "he announced there was too much bad in the world and jacked all but one of the shells from his gun, spun the cylinder, and took turns clicking that gun against our foreheads until, on the second go-around, he blew the back of his head off onto Mama's new lace curtains."

Eyeing her steadily, his voice changed from a narrator to the brutal harshness of the overseer. "You understand. There's nothing on this goddamned earth that scares me now."

In the silence that followed his speech, she heard the unmistakable metallic ker-CHUNK from under his end of the table.

Her eyes flicked down for an instant and she saw his right hand was hidden.

His unblinking drill-bit eyes bored into hers, and when she heard the thunder coming closer, she knew she'd lost.

Shakily, lifting the wineglass with her left hand, she slowly drank it down as she clipped the small gun to her leg and buttoned the placket with her right hand.

She was afraid that her cheek would twitch, her eyelid sag, her mouth tremble. She was afraid she'd go crazy in her haste to escape the awful specter of all evil that faced her, like a black furry cloud would come over the table and enfold her in black, coarse fur and make her disappear into an eternal night of bone-breaking pain.

"Good to the last drop," she said inanely, trying to recover at least her dignity, despite her mad wish to dive out the window and run like a rabbit fleeing a cougar.

Hold to it, she told herself. Steady on.

Marshaling the shreds of fortitude left to her, she said, "I've got to go before it rains."

"Tomorrow is tomorrow," he said, easing off.

"There's that big box full of money, though," she said quickly. "Whoever wins will have to be sharp and work for it."

"More than work for it," he said. "Kill for it."

As she scooted her chair back with both hands on the edge of the table, he brought his right hand up and examined the heavy silver cigar cutter in his fingers.

Slipping the end of his cheroot beneath the blade, he squeezed the lever and with the metallic ker-CHUNK, the blade slicing off the end of the cigar and returning to its open position.

"I've cut many cigars." He smiled at her. "And I've put down a lot of sharp people."

"So what's the point?" she stammered, her voice going shrill.

"The point is I work at it and I never lose. I'm no amateur playing games. I'm a real, honest-to-God killer that takes pride in his work. What the hell else is better?"

"I don't know . . ." She was ready to bawl, "I wish I did."

"Who are you?" he demanded suddenly, throwing her off-balance again.

"Nobody, not yet. I'm still looking. Still trying. And it's not easy, mister," she said, holding back tears.

"Where do you come from?"

"Chicago. Butcher Town," she replied, still holding on to the edge of the table to steady herself. "My parents both fell to the cholera when I was young. My aunt and uncle worried about me because I kept screaming in the night. Then I'd beat up the biggest bullies in school. Nobody could figure me out. I didn't have schoolmates, I had enemies . . . sort of like your town. They were all scared as hell of me. Even the teachers."

"So?" he said bluntly.

"So there I was boss. But I didn't know why. All the other girls were simpering and wiggling and giggling and I was practicing my left hook."

"Where'd you learn to shoot?"

"It doesn't make any difference. I can shoot targets well enough. It's people I have a problem with."

"That's the difference."

"But I can learn," she protested. "I mean to. I will, for damn sure."

"No, you haven't got the grit," he said. "Eugene Dred will blow you to hell if you fight him. He's a first-class gunman, but a second-class pimp."

"Who knows?" She shrugged. "Maybe I'll get lucky."

"Maybe later on you'll draw Cort." Herod grinned, pleased with the idea.

"You've got him so beat down he can't lick his upper lip. What's the fun in that?"

"He's been playin' on your sympathy?" Herod asked, amused. "Let me tell you, most dead gunfighters had a streak of sympathy in 'em."

"I'm saying what's the point of fighting somebody starved, thirsty, and kicked all to hell?" she asked, regaining some strength.

"You chop up a rattlesnake and leave his head in one piece, he'll kill you. He can't help it. That's Cort. He just don't believe it yet."

"I'm going," she said, moving around the table to pass by him. "I'm sorry. I shouldn't have come."

"It was interesting." He smiled and snapped the cigar cutter again, Ker-CHUNK.

"I'm in over my head." She nodded, disgusted with herself.

He nodded. "You're not even worth killing."

═══ 8 ═══

SHE SLEPT FITFULLY, SHOCKED BY BLAZES OF UNHOLY light when lightning struck close by, and stunned by massive thunder that followed the whiplike crack.

She fretted about her loss of nerve when the chips were down, and how he forced her to knuckle under with a damned old cigar cutter.

If she'd only touched the nubbin of a trigger, would he have sat back choking on his own blood, or did he have some trick to fend off bullets. . . .

Suppose at his end of the table he'd fixed a steel plate under the tablecloth? Suppose she'd fired and the bullet ricocheted off the plate and he'd know she meant to kill him, that she'd shot the only shell she had . . . suppose he was up there in the big house now standing on his balcony, caped arms spread out, welcoming the lightning, hauling in its energy and storing it in the back of his head. . . .

She dreamed he was laughing like a maniac at her trick gun, her attempt to gut-shoot the invincible man of iron and granite.

The Old Bank Saloon shook under the hammering lightning, and the windows rattled as the thunder blasted against them, but sometime during the night the thunder moved on easterly with the crackling rings of lightning. The turbulence, the silver and black clouds seething, the lightning strikes against mountain peaks blasting bare rock to no purpose, sent thunder back reverberating less and less. Then the shower came, bringing peace to the bloody street.

In time she slept and dreamed of the enormous graveyard, seeing the lightning strike across it like a white-hot cleaver and the dead of Redemption emerge from the smoking hillside looking lost and bewildered. Among them she glimpsed her father. He wore his gold and silver star and he was healthy and smiling, looking forward to seeing her . . .

The shower extended itself into a light rain that fell through the rest of the night, and awake at first light, she felt the need to escape from the oppressive little room and look for something more cheery.

Dressed in her golden buckskins, she donned a butternut-dyed canvas jacket and went quietly down the stairs in the graying darkness and slipped out the front door to the veranda. She heard the rain clattering on the tin canopy and saw the empty street was soaked but not churned to mud.

Staying close to the buildings, she hurried down to Ira's Worrisome Eats and went inside.

It was light and warm, just what she wanted most. She sat at the counter where a once powerful man with iron-gray hair poured a thick china mug full of coffee and set it in front of her before even saying good morning.

"Good morning, ma'am," he said, pushing the sugar bowl next to the coffee. "Wet out."

"Better than all that thunder and lightning. I thought surely it would blow up the town clock."

"No, it never does. It rocks the tower sometimes, but it leaves the clock alone. Care for some hot breakfast? Corn bread'll be coming out of the oven in a minute or two."

"With some scrambled eggs and bacon," she said, the gloom fading away. "Lived here long?" she asked.

"Long enough to remember the watermelon-eating contests we used to have the Fourth of July," he said. "We had foot races and a little parade, and the street—"

"Was covered with sweet clover," she said, joining his nostalgic enthusiasm.

"How'd you know!" He looked back at her from the stove and frowned. "I almost forgot how nice it smelled in the mornings, especially after a little rain."

"Someone mentioned it," she said, sipping at the coffee. "I'll bet little kids made up bouquets of clover blossoms for the schoolteacher."

"Yes," he said, turning the bacon and stirring the

eggs. "We even had a school and a church then. And the farmers would come to town with their cans of cream and boxes of eggs, sometimes a crate of chickens or a bunch of smoked hams and bacon sides and strings of sausage. . . .Hard to find that sort of thing anymore."

"Where did it go?"

"Farmers figured it was safer going down to Shady Bend. It's twice as far, but it's a nice little town."

Opening the oven door, he brought out a pan of golden brown corn bread, cut out a couple of blocks and put them on the plate with her bacon and eggs.

Taking her empty mug, he refilled it from the big blue coffeepot and said, "If you were looking for a nice place to settle down and raise a family, Shady Bend would be a good place to start."

"There's nothing wrong with Redemption, except there's no law," she said, buttering the corn bread and devouring the breakfast as if she'd missed supper the night before.

"That's true," he said carefully, looking over his shoulder, his voice dropping to a whisper. "But we don't talk about that. Better to talk about the weather or the olden days."

Finishing her breakfast, she looked at his once powerful shoulders bowed down, the furtive look in his eyes, the pallor of a sick spirit, and she asked quietly, "What did he do to you?"

"That's the trouble. He didn't," the slumped-down counterman said. "I had a son. When he was sixteen, he wanted to go with them. By the time he was seventeen, I couldn't hold him back. By the time he was eighteen, he lay over yonder in boot hill."

"And you never had a chance to kill Herod?" she asked, laying down a few coins and rising to her feet.

"Maybe . . ." he said, looking at the floor, "but I was always afraid. Guns are his game, not mine, and he has a way of looking at a man like he's all set to bite his head off, chew it up, and spit it back on what's left kicking on the ground."

"Thanks," she said. "It was a good breakfast."

The light rain came down steadily as she hurried back to the saloon veranda. She met no one on the street, and except for the town clock chiming eight o'clock, there was no sound anywhere except the pattering of raindrops.

Gaining the covered veranda, she sat in an oak rocking chair near the front door, rocked idly and wondered how the townsfolk could sit back and see their children destroyed year after year by that monster in the big house.

"By the time he was eighteen, he lay off yonder in boot hill. . . ."

How could they put up with it?

Fear. Fear of the gun. Fear of hanging. Fear of getting your tongue cut out, fear of losing your family . . . and she was no better. She'd been a trembling, craven coward the night before, just being near the man. She had failed and she was ashamed of her weakness. The townspeople must feel just like her—downcast, continually aware of failure, and fearing what would happen next.

She heard the clank of a dragging chain and turned to see Cort crabbing out on the porch, still manacled. His three-day growth of beard made him look more like the outlaw he was than the serene minister she'd first met.

He held a crust of bread in both hands and gnawed at it as he came forward dragging the chain that led inside.

The fresh bruises and contusions on his face made him look all the more vicious.

Looking back inside, she saw that the chain led to Ratsy, sprawled on top of the piano, a bottle still clutched in his right hand as he snored.

Cort looked at her carefully and saw the gray lines under her haggard eyes and thought she'd changed. She wasn't the same as the night before. It wasn't just the features drawn tight by the lack of sleep. It was something deep inside.

He finished the bread and waited quietly for her to speak.

"Nobody wants to shoot in the rain," she said, glancing over at him. "You need a hot, dry day to make men crazy."

"It'll let off soon enough."

"Were you just a kid—say seventeen—when you joined up with Herod?"

"About that. But I was big enough to know better. He singled me out of a crew of cowboys that'd brought a herd of cows up to Ellsworth. Just a bunch of crazy kids treeing the town, hootin', hollerin' cowboys shootin' at the moon," Cort said quietly. "We thought we were tough, and maybe we were, but we didn't know anything about bad. I guess he saw I was quick with my hands and wasn't too smart."

"What was he doing in Ellsworth?"

"He was acting marshal, meaning he'd just killed the previous marshal. He was also running all the whores and gambling in town."

"So he really wasn't the law."

"Just the opposite," Cort said. "He cared nothing for human life or property or justice."

"What happened after Ellsworth died?"

"We thought about going on west to Dodge City, but there were others like us already there. Masterson, Earps all over, Holliday. Even Wild Bill. Herod thought it would be like secondhand—the newness already worn-out. He wanted to squat on a nice new town in a territory so far away nobody cared about it."

"And it was named Redemption . . . and sweet clover grew in the streets."

"Yes." He looked at her strangely, then off at the rain dripping from the eaves. "But I never saw it like that. I went south of the border."

"Why? You have a sudden change of heart? Guilty conscience?" she asked, rocking back and forth.

"It wasn't like that. He had a lot of men scattered out along the border, and when he sent out word, they'd come and do the job with him. That time, I didn't come like he said."

"Why, though?" she snapped, exasperated by his reluctance to come out with the straight truth.

"An . . ." He sighed deeply, stared at his manacled hands and shook his head sadly. "Can you stand it?"

"Forget it!" she said hotly. "I don't need your sad story dripping with mush."

"Lady," he frowned, "you don't want my nightmares either. I can see you've got enough of your own."

"Spit it out or shut up," she said bitterly.

"You already know he's completely fearless," Cort said hesitantly. "Well, we went down into Sonora and cleaned out a bank, but the Mexicans shot us up pretty bad. We rode, him and I, as far as we could, but the Rurales were on to us and we holed up in a mission south of Tucson. He lied to the padre about how we were innocent drifters persecuted by the Rurales. The padre hated the Rurales as much as everybody else and he hid us and fed us. He was a good man."

"I can guess the rest," she said quietly.

"Not quite," Cort said miserably. "When we were strong enough to leave, Herod told me to shoot the padre. I couldn't understand why and I refused. Herod put a gun to my head and started counting down from ten."

Cort's voice broke and he buried his face in his

manacled hands for a moment, then looked at her vacantly. "So I killed the good priest. One shot to the head. Once we were clear and I could run, I ran."

"To Hermosillo," she filled in.

Cort nodded. "He kept track of me. When he took a liking to this town, he sent out the call for everybody to come. At least I didn't come."

She said nothing and waited.

"I have sinned greatly," he said huskily. "I killed one of God's chosen servants and there is no atonement. No redemption. I am damned now and for all eternity."

"So you have nothing to lose." She nodded, without betraying a sign of sympathy.

The rain tapped on the tin roof and dripped off the eaves like tears from heaven.

After a long pause he said, "Every time you kill someone, you kill a piece of yourself. Don't go down that road. Don't become like me."

"We're different," she said harshly.

"Not so much really," he said gently, and tried to touch her.

"Leave me alone!" She jerked away as if he'd hit her.

"What did he do to you?" Cort asked gently. "Tell me about it. It might help."

"What he did to me . . ." She stared off angrily, but then clamped her lips shut and turned to stare at the big house.

"Did he betray you as a child?" Cort asked tenderly, trying to reach a rapport with her. "Did he abuse you? Threaten to kill you if you talked about it? Did he just plain rape you? Did he seduce your mother, put her in a crib, kill your father? What?"

Turning away from him in a fury, she stamped down the steps to the boardwalk. Cort tried to follow, wanting to comfort her with his touch, but succeeded only in pulling Ratsy, cursing, off the piano.

Setting himself, Ratsy jerked the chain back, throwing Cort to his knees.

Ignoring the rain, she stalked up the street to the big house, and stepping inside the front gate, looked up at the tall front windows and the balcony and yelled, almost incoherent with anger, "Come on! Get on out here and fight! I've had a belly full of you! Come on out of there, mister, come on out and take your medicine!"

Madly she stalked back and forth in the front yard. Receiving no response, she pulled her .44 and shot the extended hand off the marble statue of Jesus dripping with rain.

Herod's councillors stepped out on the porch to halt the haranguing madwoman, but were called back inside.

BLAM! She shot the other hand off, sending marble fragments rattling against the porch.

"You devil! I'm ready for you, don't back out on me now!"

BLAM! Her bullet slammed between the wet eyes of the statue with such force the neck cracked and the head toppled off into the grass.

"You don't scare me with your death and damnation!" she shrieked.

From behind lace curtains Herod watched her stamping back and forth, screaming hysterically and destroying his statue. His face, hidden by the curtains, revealed a troubled mind, a hint of uncertainty—not fear—uncertainty.

Shaking his head, he turned back to his desk and said to Sergeant Quanson seated on the other side, "Well, who understands women?"

Sitting down in a heavy walnut chair, he looked across the desk at Quanson tamping Lone Jack tobacco into his burlwood pipe, even as her voice filtered through the windows.

"Come on out of your bloody fancy two-faced house, you coward!"

"Why did you ask me over here?" Quanson asked.

"I wanted the answer to a simple question: Who's paid you to challenge me?" Herod asked bluntly.

Quanson smiled, took his time lighting the pipe, and Herod waited.

"Mr. Herod, it's your Jamboree. You send out the flyers. If a gentleman adventurer such as myself comes to compete, what else do you expect?"

"Answer a question with a question," Herod said diffidently. "I'll explain it. I took it for granted Ace Hanlon was the hired gun. He was so perfect for it, but he was just a fool, a witless grandstander. You're not."

"Thank you, Mr. Herod," Quanson said easily, his voice mellifluent, his words chosen carefully. "My name is Clay Quanson. I'm a shootist. I've been favored by surviving seventeen duels, not counting Mexicans and Orientals. I am unskilled except in killing, which I have accepted as a profession for lack of anything else. It gives me no pleasure but provides for my wants. Of course, my employer is always anonymous and completely confidential. If you wish to hire me, I am at your service."

"If I hired you to go down and kill old Whiteside at the mercantile, how long would it take you to do it?"

"If you're serious, I could probably take care of it later on today."

"Why not right now?" Herod asked, eyeing the assassin.

"I've answered enough questions," Quanson said, frowning. "You're trying to box me in."

"I'll answer it for you, then. It's because you've promised him that I come first."

"May I suggest that once again you're taking a lot for granted," Quanson said, poker-faced.

"Good-bye, Sergeant Quanson." Herod stood. "When the rain quits, I'm going to make an example of you."

"I'm waiting!" Her voice shrieked through the windows, and he turned in time to see her holster the six-gun, grab up the head of Christ and lob it at his front porch.

"After you, her," Herod said, turning back to Quanson.

"I frown on killing women."

"If you see her on your way out, tell her to stop trespassing on my property or I'll have her shot," Herod said, his anger catching fire.

"I am not your messenger boy." Quanson walked out of the room.

She was gone before Sergeant Quanson stepped out on the porch.

After throwing the stone head with its dimple between the eyes at the porch, she'd stomped around, screamed, and finally, standing with her legs spread apart and her hands on her hips, yelled, "You chickenshit, gutless piss pot! I'm waitin' for you!" Then she picked up one of the marble hands, spat on the front steps, and stalked back down the street to the front porch of the Old Bank Saloon.

From the boardwalk she saw that the blind boy had set up his stand on the porch, and coming out the bat-wing doors was Scars with a glass of beer in his hand.

"Hello . . ." The boy turned, trying to identify the person coming out the door, but there was no answer. In a moment his stand started rocking back and forth, and he cried out, "Scars, don't!"

But Scars was enjoying his little joke and continued rocking the open trunk with his boot.

Trying to cover the compartments with his hands, the blind boy struggled to hold the trunk down, but there were too many little items flying off here and there as he grappled to contain the folded-out shelves.

Scars guffawed and gave the trunk a shove that sent its contents flying.

She stared at the puddle of red ink from a spilled bottle spreading over the boards, saw the blind boy tracking through it, and in her mind she saw blood.

As she mounted the steps, Scars looked at her, winked and laughed. "I'm so clumsy. I must be blind!"

Completely frustrated with her ravings in front of Herod's house, wet and miserable, she forgot all reason and in blind, red rage, swung the granite hand of Christ and smashed it in his face.

Scars fell into the spreading puddle of red ink, his right hand dragging through it.

Standing over him, she yelled, "You're goddamn right you're too goddamn clumsy, and any more of it, I'm going to blow your clumsy head off!"

Scars crawled to his feet, lost in his own rage, drawing his gun only to see that she had him covered and was one tick from squeezing the trigger.

Two councillors in tan dusters stepped out of the saloon with carbines cocked and aimed at her and Scars both.

Scars glared at her, livid with rage but aware of the carbine that had his heart dead-centered.

"Bitch," he growled.

From the other end of the porch Cort crabbed out sidewise and asked her plainly, "You going to kill someone for knocking over a stand?"

Glaring at Cort like a lioness cheated of her prey, she bit her lip and holstered the six-gun.

"That's what this town's doing to you," he warned.

Turning away, she saw the blind boy picking up the bullets and bottles of perfume, the vials of painkiller, the little packs of dried raisins, the gold pen points, the lead pencils, all the itsy-bitsy nonsense the world needed, and she stared strangely at the red ink staining the boards.

Cort saw it, and Scars saw it, but neither paid it any attention.

Suddenly she blinked her eyes and grinned.

"Hey, preacher," she said happily, "the rain's quit and it's not even noon yet. Praise the Lord."

"You're my type of lady," the Kid called up from the boardwalk. "Only a saint would praise the Lord for the killing day."

"You on the board for today?" she asked.

"Later on. I can't quite remember who it is." The Kid laughed recklessly and added, "Some poor punkin-head probably. Some clumsy half-wit that don't know any better."

"You're just teasin' me, Kid. You think you can make me so mad I'll miss you," Scars in his high-pitched voice put in.

"You're on at one o'clock, Scars?" The Kid smiled. "Well, I'll be damned! I thought it'd be some kind of contest, but with you—it ain't goin' to be any fun at all."

"I'll have five holes in you before you know you're dead," Scars said strongly.

"Damn it, Scars," she said, "you've made so many

friends in the short time you've been here, there won't be a wet eye in Redemption when the Kid blows the pie waddin' out of you."

"What the hell you talkin' about?" Scars frowned, trying to figure out if she was just joking or just being mean. "Friends is my wallet. Friends is gold pieces, and I got aplenty. Friends is two Colts and a Winchester. That's more'n you got."

"You're not fighting her, Scars," the Kid taunted the big, scarred man. "Just the six-gun tornado, and I got a whole shop full of your friends and mine, but they're like women, you got to treat 'em nice or they won't give you what you want."

"Please," Cort interrupted, "can't we talk of just simple virtues?"

"Name one, preacher." The Kid chuckled.

"Love . . ."

"Oh, hell, that's the word you use to knock up your girlfriend, then kick her out in the street," she said. "The word Eugene Dred is using to put little Katie in his crib."

"Honor—" he said, with little hope in his voice.

"Honor!" the Kid hooted. "Go on over there to Boot Hill and look at all the honorable graves. Honor is for people after they're dead, right, Preach? One of these days you'll be preachin' over my dad's grave and you'll be sayin' as to how he died like an honorable man."

"Not me," Cort said. "I would say he was the son of Satan who had no comprehension of honor or love or right or wrong or fear or courage."

"That's pretty good, Preach." The Kid chuckled. "You're smarter'n you look. My question is, do you think it can be passed on to the next generation— namely me?"

"The answer is no," Cort said. "We are not guilty and cannot be punished for the sins of our fathers."

"Silence!" came the compelling command, and she saw Herod in the middle of the street, standing tall, bull shoulders set forward, his face so suffused with rage she took a step backward as if slammed by the ferocity.

"You shall not speak of me that way!" he shouted. "I am not dead! No one here will see me to my grave. There is no Honor. There is no Love, and there is no Mercy, either. Is that understood?"

"And there is no eternal good luck either, Papa," the Kid came back at him.

"Luck is not in my lexicon, Kid," Herod said, stepping closer.

She realized that he could control that power of intimidation, that he could put the blazing ruin in his eyes, the bared teeth in his scowl, the lunge of his shoulders, the red shine of his skin—all of it was in his control.

He could light it like a trail of black powder leading to a wagonload of powder kegs, or he could damp it down, stop the burning fuse, and be persuasive and charming and that loathsome word, "loving."

"I challenge you right now!" she yelled at him loud enough for the whole town to hear.

"No! No!" Cort yelled. "I'm first!"

"Ah," Herod said, making a sad, melancholy smile, "isn't that touching? Two lovers trying to save each other from someone who simply wants to throw a party."

"Lady . . ." Cort stared at her, "you stay out of this. I don't have anything to lose . . ."

"I am not planning to lose anything," she said succinctly.

"We'll see," Herod said, shrugging. "First, I'd like to speak privately to the Kid, and then I shall drive terror into the hearts of the local citizenry by disposing of their valiant knight, Sir Sergeant Quanson."

She looked at the town clock and saw the hour hand pointing straight up and the minute hand not far behind, just crunching over to four minutes to twelve.

— 9 —

THE STREET'S SLIGHT GRADE DRAINED AWAY THE RAIN, and the gray clouds parted for the sun to brighten the sky and bring steaming vapors up from the boardwalk. She saw that the town, clean and fresh, could still be a pleasant place to live.

Even a few wisps of white clover sprang up at the edges of the boardwalk as a remembrance of when the whole street had been a sweet-smelling greensward.

The buildings were more durable and sound than the people, she thought.

"Kid," Herod called, moving his way.

"You can call me that," the Kid said, grinning, "just don't call me late to dinner."

"You wanted to make a point when you entered the contest," Herod said seriously, "and you made it. Now I'm asking you to step down. It's no disgrace, it's minding the head man."

"Why me?" the Kid asked, looking skeptically at Herod. "Blood thicker than water? You looking for to call me son, so's you'll have someone to carry on for you?"

"I was afraid you wouldn't understand," Herod said coldly, refusing to give the Kid a hint of the recognition he desperately wanted. "I want you to withdraw because you're over your head. Maybe another year and you'll understand it."

"I'll quit when you do," the Kid said, disappointed but not downcast.

"I'm telling you to wait till you grow up," Herod said strongly. "You'll have your time."

"Not while you're still around," the Kid said bitterly, stepping forward as if to crowd Herod aside, his bright blue eyes holding Herod's.

Herod didn't budge. He knew the Kid would accept him as his father, and more than that, be a good son, minding his manners and helping all he could, but Herod would give nothing to the Kid and resented his closeness.

"Don't ever cross me, Kid," Herod growled, his features hard as granite, "and don't ever try to stare me down like you're doing now! I don't need you, Kid. I'm not old or sick, and you're not half the man I am. You never will be!"

The Kid's right leg shifted slightly forward and spread out a bit to give him better balance, and his right hand touched the hard leather holster on his thigh.

From down the street Horace, unaware of their quarrel, called out, "Take your positions, please!"

"Saved by the referee." The Kid chuckled.

Herod pushed him out of the way, feeling better because the Kid was provoked enough by now to stay in the contest to the bitter end.

At the other end of the street, beyond Horace, Sergeant Quanson stepped out from the crowd and faced Herod.

"Round Two!" Horace announced portentously, enjoying the chance to officiate. It made him feel as if he controlled the contest and all the people, too, as if it were his show and he must make sure everything went smoothly, orderly, and fairly.

"Four fights today!" He held up four fingers to emphasize the point. "Featuring the most talented, tenacious and top-ranked trigger twisters of the century! The winner will be the contestant left standing—"

"Left alive," Herod rasped, cutting across Horace's grandiloquence.

Horace looked at Herod nervously and saw no change or retraction.

"Last alive!" he called out, and setting his rubbery face, he declared, "From now on we fight to the death!"

"You're changing the rules!" Cort yelled from the saloon porch.

"Any problem with that?" Herod called out to Sergeant Quanson.

The black gunman, lean, wiry, and lethal, his shaven head gleaming in the sunlight, shrugged his shoulders and replied, "I was planning on killing you anyways. After that we'll change the rules back again."

"God damn it!" Herod snarled. "I'm sick up to my ears with cheap back-talk!"

"Gentlemen, your fate is in your hands. Take your positions, please!"

Herod ignored the barman and walked a circle to ease off the futile anger. Everybody was getting to be so goddamned unruly and smart-ass, despite his efforts to give them a great Jamboree. He thought he just might call it off next year.

He heard the old clock grunt and clunk and heard the telltale tick just before the hand flicked up and the chime struck.

BLAM!

Herod's speed made Sergeant Quanson look like a sleepwalker. Before he'd even curled his fingers around the butt of his Peacemaker, Herod's bullet spun through his intestines.

Not bothering to look at Quanson fall to one knee with a quizzical look on his shining face, Herod turned a slow circle, addressing the whole town loud and clear.

"I'm confused!" He cracked the whip in his voice, and the townspeople, seeing their champion down, wished they'd never heard of Quanson.

"All I hear from you all yellow-gutted, jelly-headed cowards is how poor you are. How you can't afford my fees and taxes and my protection! I try to be nice to you, try to protect you, and this is what I get!" Herod's voice deepened into the power of an artillery barrage, and facing away from Quanson, he tried to include the whole town in his speech.

Quanson, holding his left arm over his abdomen, slowly regained his feet. With sweat beading his face, he set his mind on clutching the grip of his swiveled .44 and at least dying even.

As his weary hand touched the butt of the Peacemaker, Herod continued.

"You show me your empty pockets, your patched raggedy-ass clothes, your hungry children . . . and yet somehow, you've all found enough money to hire a professional assassin to kill me!"

Whirling, Herod snapped a shot at Quanson, his bullet striking the barrel of his quick-draw rig, spinning the Peacemaker like a wheel of fire. The force of the bullet turned Quanson aside and he staggered backward a step.

Not pausing in his harangue, Herod went on angrily. "Well, where does all this money come from? What am I to think? Is there a problem with arithmetic? If you've got so much to throw away on a piss-poor gunfighter, I'm just going to have to take some more from you . . . 'cause you clearly have forgotten the message. . . ."

Herod paused for effect, and taking a deep breath,

roared out, "THIS IS MY TOWN! IF YOU LIVE TO SEE THE DAWN, IT'S BECAUSE I HAVEN'T KILLED YOU IN THE NIGHT! I AM BOSS OF EVERYTHING, AND EVERY DAY I DECIDE WHO LIVES . . . AND WHO DIES!"

Ashen-faced, the townspeople hung their heads and winced under the lashes of his speech.

Furtively they looked at Sergeant Quanson, their last tiny flickering flame of hope. Quanson still struggled to keep his knees locked, his midsection from spilling out his juices. If he could just get his right hand on the gun butt and elevate the barrel ninety degrees . . . if he just had two seconds . . .

But Herod was done talking and tired of playing with Quanson. In a tenth of a second he sent his third bullet through Quanson's throat, turned back to the crowd and growled, "There goes all your savings down the drain."

The townsfolk studied their patched boots, knowing he was right and their last hope was gone.

A wave of thunder rolled across the valley, the clouds closed in overhead, and the crowd along the street looked up at the sky anxiously.

The clock said two minutes to one, and the Kid, waiting in the street, yelled anxiously, "Where's Horace? Get him out here before it starts raining again!"

Tall, hulking Scars slouched indolently on down the street. Wearing only a cowhide vest over his upper torso, the scars and tattoos which he prided himself on were fully revealed. Cocking his right arm, he flexed his biceps, which in turn made the naked lady on his arm do the hoochy-koochy.

Rain or shine made no difference to him. All he wanted was another hash mark on his left arm.

He knew the Kid was fast, but Scars didn't think he was tough. He'd never rooted through a Saturday night in El Paso. He'd never fought in a range war. He'd never hired out as a soldier in a Mexican revolution. He'd never done time. So, he hadn't learned all the tricks of the trade.

Maybe he's fast, he thought, watching the tattoo lady wiggle her butt on his arm, so maybe I throw mud in his eyes. Maybe I fall and play dead and shoot him while he's doin' his dance. Maybe I do the hat trick—

Horace stepped out into the street and drew himself up importantly, cleared his throat and announced, "Rain or shine, this fight commences on the stroke of one! Get yourselves set, it's Scars against the Kid, so let the thunder ro-o-o-ll!"

The clock showed one minute before the hour, and Horace hurried off the street.

Facing the Kid, Scars liked the idea of the hat trick. First your left hand goes to your hat and sends it sailing off to the left, at the same time you whirl to the right, draw, fire! The sailing hat always slowed down the hot guns, because it threw them off their practiced routines.

174

He heard the iron grumble in the clock tower, extended his left hand, heard the telltale tick, and a hair ahead of the chime his hat went sailing off to the left, his feet executed the whirl perfectly, even as his six-gun came up to pick up the Kid, and then it all went to hell.

The Kid's draw was a thing of beauty, if you could see it. Smoothly flowing and fast as a green racer, his first shot took Scars in the chest, puffing dust from the cowhide vest. Just for the hell of it, he punched his second shot through the still sailing hat.

Scars lurched backward, his six-gun firing high, and then his knees gave way and he tipped over slowly, the way a tall pine tree falls.

The Kid fell to his knees in joy. Pounding the wet street with his left hand, he laughed and cried out, "Is it possible? Is it possible to improve on perfection?!"

Even as Charlie Moonlight dragged Scars's body off to one side of the street to Doc Wallace, the Kid rose and played to the crowd.

"I *heard,* I *heard* him move his hand! And him thinkin' I'd fall for the old hat trick! I'm on a different level! Another world!" The Kid looked over at Herod and taunted, "I am the new mayor of this town!"

"Heart shot," Doc Wallace called out. "The Kid wins."

"Children don't play with guns, and grown men beware!" the Kid yelled as Mattie Silk, her blond curls bobbing like coils of brass, ran out and hugged him, and the rain suddenly broke loose, ending the entertainment.

Horace yelled from the saloon porch, "No more fights till it clears up some."

Charlie Moonlight made the effort to drag Scars's body up under the tin awning of his carpentry shop out of the rain. The body still trembled and twisted in spasms, and he watched the naked lady wiggle her butt and rotate her tits until she got cold.

Lightning cracked off in the hills and the thunder came rolling again as she stepped inside the crowded saloon, which stank stronger than a wolf's den, she thought, as the damp unwashed bodies and wet filthy clothes released their concentrated stenches into the steaming atmosphere.

The strange mood of the crowd bothered her. Instead of a bunch of half-drunk gunfighters rehashing the Scars-Kid fight, there was a subdued intensity of speech, as if they were saying one thing and thinking something else.

"Good shooting," she said to the Kid, and seeing Horace behind the bar trying to pour drinks and look at the stairway at the same time, she asked quietly, "What the hell's wrong with him?"

"I don't know if it's wrong, but it's sure too bad." The Kid glanced up the stairway. "Little Katie's some slow. . . ."

She heard them over the tense constrained voices, the playful resistance, the giggle, the rattle of bedsprings, the tiny wail and the guttural purring of Eugene Dred, and she felt sick.

Turning back to the Kid, she snapped, "You goin' to stand for that?"

"I reckon it's done," the Kid said, unsmiling. "He waited till everybody was outside—and like I said, she's a little slow. . . ."

"But Horace?" she muttered, unable to say what she meant.

"Listen, lady," the Kid said seriously, "Horace knows Dred is a killer that kills people he don't have to, and he's got a temper if anybody tries to get in his way."

"There's fifty people in this room and not a goddamned one of them gives a damn about that girl!" she said bitterly. "I could throw up."

"Let me buy us a bunch of them Dead-Eyes." The Kid put on his smile. "We'll try that dynamite bed again, and this time for sure, you'll get a big blast."

"Maybe later." She felt alone and a little sad.

Upstairs a door opened and a disheveled Katie came out weeping small sobs as tears washed down her cheeks.

Seeing the crowd in the bar, she ran down the stairs and on out into the rain.

Seconds later Eugene Dred strolled along the upstairs landing, smoothing down his coat and trousers. A look of contented amusement crossed his face as he leisurely came down the staircase. Seeing Ratsy hanging onto Cort's chair, he murmured smugly, "Nice . . . With a little ambition, she'll do fine."

Even Ratsy didn't look him in the face, and as he strolled on across the room, Dred caught her angry eyes and sneered.

Contemptuously brushing past her, he sat down at the poker game with his back to her.

"Deal me in," Dred said. "This is my lucky day."

She looked over toward Horace, hoping he'd bring up a ten-gauge greener and start blasting, but he was looking at the floor shamefaced.

She knew it was his affair and that she should stay out of it. But she still couldn't stand to be identified with these shabby no-good, worthless sonsabitches who would do nothing, not even say a mumbling word. You were either something or nothing, she thought. If you were something, you did something.

Even then she might have cooled off and let it go, because by now the harm was done, but Dred looked around the table with smarmy pride and smirked. "Had her jerking and squealing like a pig caught under a gate."

Without thinking, she grabbed Dred by the hair and jerked him back over his chair so that his knees upset the card table and the poker players hunted for shelter.

Smashing him to the floor, she slammed her boot to the side of his head.

Clutching his bleeding ear, he rolled sidewise, and aware now of what had happened, he got quickly to his feet as she made a rush at him and flailed away at his moldy face. Charging through her fists, he grabbed her by the throat with both hands and tried to wrestle her to the floor. She stamped her heel hard into his instep, and he slammed her against the wall.

Bystanders came into the action, grabbing Dred by his neck and shoulders and pulling him away from her, while others made a wall she couldn't penetrate, yelling, "No more! Break it up! No fighting here, take it someplace else!"

"Out on the street! Right now!" she screamed at him.

"You're goddamned right, you split-tail morphy-dyke!" he yelled back at her, the pockmarks on his face white pits against the choleric red.

Horace and the Kid stayed with her, keeping her from attacking the gaudily dressed whoremaster, while three lesser gunmen stayed with Dred.

"He draws crossways," the Kid said. "Seeing it for the first time might rattle you some."

"Kill that sonofabitch, lady, and I'll give you anything you want," Horace said.

"I'm taking what I want," she said angrily, hurrying into the street. "I'm not waiting around for somebody to give it to me."

Outside, rain rattled on the tin roof, pelting down with such force she was blinded until she cocked her hat forward to protect her eyes.

"Don't aim at his head or legs or anything," Cort called out sharply. "Just aim for the middle. This rain will throw you off a lot. Just shoot for the middle and you'll hit something."

With the cacophony of the downpour mingling with the massive thunder battering the street, she could hardly comprehend the advice her well-wishers were offering.

For her, the important thing was to keep her righteous rage afire, because she believed nothing could stand in the way of it.

Eugene Dred appeared in the street and faced her.

Horace yelled, "Go at it!" and fled to the board-walk.

Lightning popped close by. In the garish flash was the stark vision of the tall gunman, his two guns under his arms protruding butt first, facing the lady in buckskins.

As the lightning flash vanished, Dred drew with his right hand the Colt .44 from under his left arm and fired. He fired rapidly as he marched forward, but his aim was off. The range was too far in the driving rain, and she did not fire until she'd taken three steps forward, and then, taking Cort's advice, aimed at the belly of Dred's pink shirt, fired and missed.

Shouting at his bodyguards, John Herod ran down the front steps of his house, still putting on an oiled canvas coat.

Dred's .44 clicked on empty and, with a quick draw with his left hand, fired once with his other revolver, and not satisfied, he border-shifted, tossing the Colt over to his right hand and, peering through the rain, took aim and fired again.

She felt the whip of the bullet nick her cheek, and once more tried to sight in the pink shirt just above the silver and turquoise belt buckle. They were closer now, not ten paces apart. As she squeezed the trigger, the .44 bucked in her hand, and Eugene Dred staggered backward.

She saw from the bloom of blood in his groin that she'd shot low. She lifted her Colt to fire again. The hammer fell on a spent shell and she drew her other Colt, wet and slick, with her left hand, ready to fire point-blank at his mouth, opened wide with horror, his yellow horse teeth bared as the shock hit him.

Sinking to his knees, he clutched at his jellied genitals and cried out, "That's not fair!"

She stared at him, the Colt a foot from his liver-colored face, and felt the sneaky pleasure of killing seep through her body and brain and on to her trigger finger.

Why not? He deserves it. He fired first. He drew first blood. He should be killed to make the world a better place. Go ahead, end his suffering, blow his fucking brains out!

"Kill him," Herod said, coming up beside her.

Herod's voice countered her murderous temptation, and she saw the ruined man then as a human being who had been punished enough, emasculated, gelded, for all his bright plumage, hardly more than a pet canary now.

Lowering the hammer gently, she holstered the Colt and dabbed at the scratch across her cheek.

"He's down," she said dully, the fire that had burned so hotly seconds before now sinking away into coals.

"You've got to finish him off," Herod said. "That's the rule."

She hadn't the strength to tell him to take his rule and piss up a rope. Dumbly, she turned away.

Her hat brim sagged under the weight of the rain and a rivulet poured down over her eyes.

Not stopping, she walked back toward the porch of the saloon, no longer sure of her rightness and uncertain of her righteousness.

She saw a blurred figure come running at her and she held up a hand to ward off what might have been a blow, but it was the small, chunky form of a drenched Katie weeping and howling and wailing. "You shot him! O dear Lord, you shot Gene! It's my fault! Oh my God, I'm sorry!"

"Make up your mind," she said. "It's your life."

"I don't know . . . I don't want anybody hurt!" Katie blubbered. "He said a lot of nice things to me . . . he wasn't all bad. . . ."

"Don't be so goddamned dumb," she said. "It won't be the last time you hear a line of bullshit. Next time, though, use your head."

It was wasted, she thought. The girl had not enough brains to know the truth and joy of mating, but would blunder on, too foolish to trouble her head by understanding responsible reality, bringing disaster with her charms wherever she went.

I wasn't wrong, she thought, I just wasn't right,

either. Still, I marked that sonofabitch. Then she realized that she could have been as foolish as Katie at that age. She could have played the giggle game with someone that looked like a flamboyant buccaneer eager to carry her away to paradise.

Women will believe anything if the man tells them they're pretty, she thought. That's all it takes. Every morning and every evening they'll tell you you're pretty, and then they'll tell you to just lie back, some friends of yours are coming over for a good time.

Damn it to hell, she said to herself, either way, we're screwed.

Empty of emotion and downcast, she gained the porch and felt her sodden blouse clinging to her breasts and she shivered from the cold.

"The contest is not over yet!" Herod snarled at her back.

Turning her head, she glared at him. "For me it is," and with the gun still in her hand, moved on into the saloon.

"Give me a drink," she said to Horace, trembling now from the wet cold.

"On me." He looked at her as if trying to express his thanks.

"Skip the olive," she said. Laying the gun on the bar, she lifted the glass with her left hand and drank down half the rye whiskey.

As she took the glass from her lips and looked at it gratefully. BLAM! The glass exploded.

Beyond surprises by now, her right hand slapped down to the Colt on the bar and she whirled, the muzzle of the gun swinging to target pale-faced Eugene Dred in the doorway. Quicker than she could ever explain, her finger touched the trigger the same instant her eyes touched his, and in the same instant his craggy jaw split into a ragged rat hole and he collapsed backward.

In an instant he was there, and in that same instant he was not there.

"Holy Jesus, lady!" Horace whispered, coming up from behind the bar.

"Give me the bottle," she said, her teeth chattering, her whole body quaking not just from the cold, but from the raw ferocity of her emotions.

Horace put the half-full bottle of rye in front of her, and with her left hand she tilted up the bottle and swallowed twice.

"I'm cold," she said, holstering the six-gun. "I've got to change into dry clothes."

Upstairs, she changed quickly, reloaded her six-guns, and carrying her canvas coat, she walked downstairs again.

Meeting her at the bottom, the Kid searched her face with a mixture of sympathy and anxiety. Touching the cut on her cheek, he said softly, "That's all right. It'll heal, but what about you?"

"I wish I knew," she said shakily, knowing it was no longer the cold that trembled inside her.

Walking to the door, she pushed through and saw the thieves and human vultures working over the sodden figure of Eugene Dred.

His nankeen pants were too ruined to steal, but his

boots were gone, as well as the sky-blue silk frock coat and open-throated pink silk shirt.

The gold-tooth man was kneeling over, trying to find something of value in Dred's ruined mouth. Frustrated, he looked up at her and growled, "You ruined a hundred dollars worth of solid gold, hand-carved teeth, lady."

Doc Wallace closed his black leather bag as she passed, and rumbled, "Where are you going?"

"Away. I'm done."

She stopped by the edge of the awning and slipped into her canvas coat.

"I've got to talk to you," he whispered, not looking at her.

"I'm going to look for a grave."

"Dear lady!"

She heard Herod's familiar voice and turned to face him. Now wearing a wool coat and carrying a black silk umbrella, he looked warm as a toad and cheery as a bottle of port wine.

"Congratulations, my dear." Herod smiled. "You have moved up to the third round!"

═══ 10 ═══

THE RAIN FALLS EQUALLY UPON THE RICH AND THE poor, the young and the old, and the quick and the dead, she thought as she watched the downpour from the open double door of the livery barn.

Strange how it starts all of a sudden on a gust of wind and will come down steady for hours and hours as if it were being measured out, then with another little gust of wind, it quits.

Summer showers, they call it. In the spring it's rain and in the winter it's snow, and it's probably all the same water evaporating from the land and condensing in the sky to fall again to rise again.

She touched the cut on her cheek and felt the scab already forming.

Waiting for the shower to pass on, she wondered if there was a larger pattern set maybe in the stars where this going and coming, living and dying, heating and cooling, growing and rotting, drying and raining, loving and hating—there was that "loving" word again—for sure it was the foundation of the pattern, even if nobody knew what it meant and most everyone used it for the wrong reasons. Still, loving was there in the plan, a tremendous invisible force that drove mankind crazy and yet could make living sublime.

And revenge? She wondered how revenge fitted into the pattern of love and rain and growth. The quick and the dead, that's where revenge fitted. As the rain suddenly ceased, its patter on the barn roof silent, the air was rain-rinsed and rich as brandy, and she thought, Tomorrow no matter what, I'll have won or lost, and I'll be either with the quick or with the dead.

Mounting up on her black gelding, she rode down the wet trail toward the river under the trees that still quietly dripped idle raindrops like wasted afterthoughts.

Coming around the curve of the bluff, she turned off to the left and rode through a ramshackle gate where some joker had put up a sign: REMAINS OF REDEMPTION.

There were many monuments, but most were inconsequential headboards driven into the ground to indicate a certain space was being used, that it would be better to dig your grave elsewhere in earth not yet occupied.

Many of the headboards, stakes, and rock slabs

carried no names or dates, being nothing more than markers, which by the time they fell and rotted away, the remains they were marking would have returned to the earth as well.

Dismounting, she walked through the maze. A few of the stones bore chiseled names but none she recognized. A few had been sculpted into stone crosses or sleeping lambs or crude angels, as if they could stubbornly represent a standard of niceness or normality in a cemetery of godless chaos, tumult, and death.

Not the somber sky nor the wet earth wearied her spirit, it was this hillside full of nameless corpses rotting back to earth that made her want to keen and weep. They'd all had mothers and fathers and perhaps children, but where was the love and the hate, the remembrance and revenge, the quick and the dead?

Where had it gone?

The name she sought was not there. It had not been penciled on a board or scratched on a chunk of limestone.

Oh, rain, come hard, come forty days and forty nights and wash this grievous shame away, she prayed with her eyes closed.

A raptoral claw seized her shoulder and she almost screamed as the seamed, haggard face of Doc Wallace appeared before her eyes.

She took a step backward in instinctive horror, but he held her arm and asked, "You remember?"

She nodded. "Then you know who I am."

"Of course." He wheezed and coughed weakly into his hand. "I brought you into this sorry world and I put you on an eastbound coach a long time ago. Where have you been?"

"I've been everywhere and done nothing."

Gently drawing her close, he put his arms around her and murmured, "I knew it wouldn't be easy. You were so small . . ."

The sorrow she felt for that little girl whose happiness had been torn from her almost overflowed from her heart, but she bit her lip and forced herself to think of the man she meant to kill.

"Your father—" the old man murmured.

"I can't talk about it—" she said tightly, stepping away, her face hard.

"You've been looking for his grave," he said, his black nail-head eyes on hers.

"Yes," she admitted. "There's not a trace."

"I tried . . ." he said, shaking his head, "but Herod wanted nothing for people to remember. Your father's body was wrapped in canvas, weighted with stones and dumped in the river."

Her mind fired at this ultimate insult and her fists clenched in anger.

"The hog. The stinking boar hog . . ." she gritted out.

"There are still good people here," he said quietly, "but they're beat down into cowards like me. They've been waiting for someone decent to stand up against Herod . . ."

She saw the pattern then: "waiting for someone

decent," yes, decent and suicidal! It was in the pattern that the decent, like her father, would rise and stand against evil, and it was in the pattern that the decent would then be martyred by the supreme power of evil amiably doing its job.

"I thought I could do it," she said dully.

"You're the only one . . ." he said, "but it's not for me to say."

"I can't do it!" she cried out. "I can't kill him! I've had my chances, but I'm too scared. I don't know how, but he's got more nerve than I have. Maybe I'm more scared of dying than he is. . . ."

With palsied hands he pulled out an old metal badge, a silver and gold star. The silver was crusted with black from fire and the gold points bent and blunted.

"Child," the old doctor put the badge in her hand, "you've been dead ever since it happened. You're more scared of living."

"Thanks for saving this, Doc." She held the badge with both hands. "I wanted something of his I could touch."

"I hope it helps some," he said, his voice quavering, his nail-head eyes on her.

"You pulled me off the street when they rode in . . ." she murmured. "Why you?"

"Your mother died two years before from the cholera," he said. "Your dad and me and some others in town were taking care of you . . ."

"Then I killed my father . . ." she said weakly.

"It wasn't you. It wasn't your fault! Herod was

going to kill your daddy no matter what. When he caught you, he just made a more cruel game of it. It pleases him to force weaker people to do terrible, perverse things."

"I can't forget it. It's with me night and day."

"I'd hoped . . . even though I knew you'd never forget, could never recover . . . I'd hoped you'd come back and somehow put an end to it." He patted her shoulder. "But if you can't, you'd best leave right now."

"There's a man back there . . ." she said thoughtfully, "the man named Cort . . ."

"He's another one forced to do perverse acts against his will and conscience." Doc shook his head. "He's helpless."

"But maybe between the two of us . . . ?"

"Child, leave it be. Try to start over!" the Doc said fearfully. "Herod has some devilish scheme, and you're the intended sacrifice."

"I've got to give it another try. . . ." She slipped the badge into her vest pocket. Mounting the black, she paused a moment and added, "Don't bury me here, Doc."

As she rode back toward town, Doc turned to look at the serried ranks of markers and muttered to himself.

"If only evil would die, if only it could be killed and buried and be forgotten . . ."

Sighing, shaking his head, he climbed into the buggy and started his horse back toward the barn.

She was rubbing down the black when the Kid

entered the barn and asked anxiously, "You're not leaving?"

"Not yet. Why?"

"I was afraid you'd gone. I know this sounds dumb, but I really care about you," the Kid stammered nervously. "I mean, I know it's a bad time to talk romantic, but—"

"Why do you live like this?" she suddenly exploded. "How can you stand it?"

"Stand what?" He eyed her, puzzled, not understanding her anger. "This is my dad's town, not mine . . ."

"What's the difference?" she came back at him hotly. "Would you make it any better if you took over—or would you just take forty percent instead of fifty?"

The Kid backed away, not comprehending what she was talking about, and not wanting to know. He didn't even want to think about it. "You're a strange one—a regular worrywart." He smiled.

"Kid," she said, letting off, seeing she couldn't dent his good-natured complacency, "get out of this town. Go see the world and then come back."

"You and me." He grinned. "Maybe after I've won the Jamboree, you can show me the sights."

As she started for the open stable doors, he added, "Better run, that preacher is due to fight right soon."

Leaving him behind, she hurried toward the main street. Suddenly she caught herself and asked: Why? What's the rush? Where's the fire? That man doesn't mean anything to you or you to him. He's just another one of Herod's victims.

Forcing herself to slow down, she came to the main square and turned toward the porch of the saloon.

She saw that Horace had just finished his announcement and that the clock hands stood at one minute to two. Down the street waited the giant Indian in his black suit. In his hair were two eagle feathers and around his neck hung a bear-claw necklace with extra silver, turquoise, and red coral beads.

Across from her, Cort stood with his ankles still chained together. Shaking his head, he seemed to be saying that he would not draw, would not fight.

"Do or die!" Herod yelled at him from his private bench, and gestured at the three riflemen in tan dusters standing on the roofs.

"Where have you been?" the blind boy asked. "The Kid was asking—"

"Can that Indian shoot?" she asked, ignoring the question.

"He wouldn't be out there if he couldn't," the boy said, and selecting a cartridge from his trunk shelf, he commenced working it through his fingers nervously. "Same as that Cort."

"He doesn't want to be out there."

"I'm not so sure. . . ." the blind boy said. "I heard he tried to reform but killin's already in his blood."

The clock workings growled and Cort heard the

tip-off tick before the chime struck. Slowly he went through the motions of drawing the .44.

Spotted Horse drew incredibly fast, and without hesitating, pointed his weapon and fired.

The bullet tore a line across the top of Cort's head, the hair ripped from his scalp, leaving a white welt and a thin line of oozing blood. Half an inch lower and his skull would have been split open.

Feeling the burning pain and seeing the big Indian step forward aiming for a kill shot, Cort fired quickly, loosing a bullet that smashed into Spotted Horse's broad chest, shattering the ornate necklace and slamming him backward to the street.

All was hushed as Doc Wallace stepped out to check the fallen man.

"He's as good as dead," Doc croaked, and there was a murmur of disapproval from the crowd.

Spotted Horse coughed and trembled. Blood ran from his mouth and he turned his face to retch.

Herod frowned. "He's got to be killed dead."

Spotted Horse passed his left hand over his mouth and fingered out a mashed soft lead bullet. Squinting at it dazedly, he rolled to his side, slipped the bullet into his coat pocket and struggled to his feet.

Still gripping the .44 in his right hand, he grinned at Cort, his lips smeared with blood. Taking another step forward, he lifted his weapon.

Cort looked over at Herod and yelled, "Give me another bullet."

The crowd started to chant, "KILL HIM! KILL

HIM! KILL HIM!" as the Indian took another step forward, his six-gun raised and ready.

"I explained the rules very carefully, Cort. You've got to kill your man." Herod smiled tensely, his eyes sucking in the presence of death.

Spotted Horse jerked the trigger and fired. The bullet whined by Cort's ear, and as the Indian took another long step forward, Cort yelled at the crowd, "SOMEBODY GIVE ME A SHELL!"

"I will not kill!" Herod chuckled, taunting the frantic preacher. "That's what you told me. 'I have renounced violence.'"

Spotted Horse's next bullet kicked up dust between Cort's legs, and Cort faced Herod and, trying to goad him into action, yelled, "Afraid to face me, Herod? Scared you'll find out who's best?"

"I know who's best," Herod growled, unmoving.

Frantically, she tried to punch a cartridge out of the loop of her gun belt, but the shell, stuck in the tight leather, wouldn't budge.

Spotted Horse took his time lifting the six-gun, and the blind boy, tossing his cartridge toward Cort, yelled, "Here!"

Cort's fingers snatched the shell out of the air, rammed it into the open cylinder, and as Spotted Horse carefully squeezed the trigger, Cort's own gun bloomed. A red pit appeared on the broad, bronze forehead, and Spotted Horse slowly fell sidewise like a blasted mountain.

A gasp rose from the crowd as Spotted Horse lifted

his hand toward his head as if he might extract the slug and arise again, but the effort was too much. The hand slowly fell back to the ground in final defeat.

Cort stood staring incredulously at the body, then felt a surge of emotion. More than simple relief, there was a sense of triumphal joy in it, and he despised his spirit for betraying him.

Ratsy came forward and snapped the manacles around Cort's wrists. The crowd yelled insults, and only a smiling Herod clapped his hands slowly and called out, "Well done!"

Horace importantly stepped out into the street and announced, "The second day's contests are now officially over with. The finals start at noon tomorrow. Let the Jamboree roll!"

Herod rose from the bench and approached Cort with a smile. Suddenly seizing Cort's clerical collar, he ripped it off savagely, tearing his shirt open as well. Tossing the torn collar into the mud, he said, "Welcome back, killer."

Cort looked at his open gun hand and shook his head in shame.

"How did you know where to throw that shell?" she asked the blind boy as Ratsy led Cort off the street.

"He never moved from where he started," the boy said. "Why didn't you throw him one?"

"Damn shells been in my belt so long they're stuck."

"A few drops of neat's-foot oil will fix that, lady,"

the boy said, fingering through the compartments of his trunk, and finding the vial of oil, handed it to her.

"How much?"

"Nothing. You overpaid me yesterday."

"I meant to," she said, and dropped a ten-dollar gold piece in his cup.

"Thanks, ma'am."

"Doc ever look at your eyes?"

"Yes, but not soon enough," the boy said.

"What was the matter?"

"My ma worked some for Eugene Dred and caught something before I was born. It ruined my eyes," he said matter-of-factly. "She didn't last very long."

"Who raised you, then?" she asked, frowning.

"Doc Wallace got some of the folks to help. There's some good ones in this town even if you never notice them."

"Goddamn it—" she muttered bitterly.

"Lady, make no mistake about it, I'd rather be alive and blind than just plain dead. I'm doing good enough, and soon as somebody turns this town around, I'll do a lot better."

"That's why you threw Cort the cartridge!" she exclaimed, understanding now that he had his own solid reasons for keeping Cort alive.

"He might could do it," the boy said wistfully. "He might."

"You don't think I can?" she asked.

"You went up to the big house last night, and Herod was still pulling the strings this morning," the boy said simply.

"I was afraid—plain out scared," she said, close to
pleading for understanding and sympathy. "I meant
to, but he had too much . . ."

"Control?" the boy offered.

"Controlled power," she said. "It was like—"

"Thunder and lightning," he put in with a small
smile. "You're forgetting I was born here. I know
him better than anybody thinks because he never
notices me. He takes it for granted I'm harmless.
Like I don't know nothing."

"You know anything special?" she asked, wondering what he was driving at.

"He don't like surprises. He likes to know where
every card in the deck is, and he wants 'em all to be
laid out exactly the way he planned it."

"That's part of his control."

"Yes, because he can't handle surprises," the boy
said.

She thought the boy was making sense, but she
didn't see how it could be of any practical help to
her. Looking around, she was suddenly aware the
street was very quiet.

"Where'd everybody go?" she asked, puzzled.

"Most of them went into the saloon," he said. "I
don't know about Cort. Ratsy's been talking about
putting him in a show over at the whorehouse."

"Cort!" she shrieked.

"There's something about chains and—and—
and . . ."

"Sex," she put in quickly.

"That attracts violent men," the boy said quietly.

She didn't wait to think it over. He heard her suck in a deep breath and clatter down the boardwalk before he'd finished talking.

"It's fixin' to storm again," he said aloud.

WHAM! The door with the etched-glass oval pane set in it slammed open and she stepped inside. Flocked purple wallpaper covered the walls of what had once been the hotel vestibule, where once travelers rustled periodicals and exchanged half-truths of where they were from, what they had been doing, where they were going, and what expectations they had for what they intended to do.

She stared around at the threadbare furniture, the horsehide sofa covered by a blanket to hide gaping holes. The spittoons were arranged carefully to save the rug, but never carefully enough for spitters cock-eyed from drink. The old counter where the register book had been was turned into a small bar which featured rare, exotic liquors brewed in the cellar. Crème de menthe, crème de cacao, crème de this and that, all meant for the sporters to order at three dollars a shot. Bottles labeled Old Crow and Old Yellowstone had been refilled with forty rod colored by adding burned sugar.

The room reeked from spilled drinks, cat functions, old tobacco spit, vomitings of drunks long since dead, and an overlayer of cheap perfume which was sprayed about when the basic ineluctable stink became too overpowering.

She wanted to clamp her nose shut and run

outside for a breath of rain-freshened air, but there wasn't time. Glaring around the room, she saw Mattie Silk, cuddling up on the Kid's lap, a few fat and busty whores with dyed hair, dressed in sateen ruffles, red or purple, and a few gaunt, hollow-cheeked sporters looking as if they'd hard-wintered. Powdered, rouged, and mascaraed, clad in sateen skirts that hid their lean shanks and blouses amplified with many ruffles and bows to conceal the ribby chests and bedraggled bosoms, all lounging around with a variety of gunfighters no better looking than the whores they were trying to bargain down to a free ash-dumping.

"Where is he?" she snapped at the half-drunk Kid, whose head drooped over Mattie's enchanting bosom.

"You're in the wrong place," Mattie said. "We ain't takin' on any new hands till we know who's boss."

"I'm not lookin' to turn a trick, sweetie," she said, "I'm lookin' for my man."

Mattie thought about it for a second and, puzzled, asked, "Ratsy?"

"No, she means that preacher," the Kid said, waking up. "Cort what's-his-name."

"They all up yonder," Mattie said. "They's a show I don't need to see."

She charged up the stairs two at a time to the hallway. She tried a locked door, then kicked it open.

A naked graybearded man on his knees with a pair

of fat legs dangling over his shoulders looked up, surprised.

She charged on to the next door and found another weird scene she wanted to forget immediately, and charged on to the third door.

Ratsy, Dick O'Toole, Simp Dixon, and a heavily bandaged Dog Kelly were holding the manacled Cort down on a rumpled bed while a naked, crinkly-haired blond whore knelt between his spread-out legs, undoing the buttons of his pants as he struggled against his chains.

"HOLD IT!" she snarled, drawing her .44.

A frozen tableau. The drunken gunmen staring at her. The bought and paid for woman gripped in fear. Cort's face shifting from shame to—what . . . gratitude?

"Move out," she said. "He's mine."

"Lady," Ratsy protested, his voice slurring, his mind barely comprehending, "lady, see—I'm in charge, you know—in charge . . . of this prisoner, and you better not—better not, get in the way . . ."

"Get out of here!" She stepped forward and laid the muzzle of her Colt on Ratsy's right eye.

"Go," she whispered.

"Yes'm," Ratsy said, "but don't turn him loose—"

Slowly she cocked the revolver and said, "One . . ."

The yellow-headed, hawk-faced whore was the first. Grabbing up an armful of clothing, she fled the room, while the four men were more surly and reluctant.

"Goddamn you!" she snarled. "Now!"

Slow or fast, they were too turgid for her mood, and she leaped forward and struck Dog Kelly on the side of the head with the heavy-barreled Colt.

His anger and hatred faded as his eyes rolled up and he fell to the floor.

"All right, lady, all right, all right, all right . . ." Ratsy chattered, and with O'Toole and Dixon, dragged Dog Kelly out of the room.

After closing the door and setting a chair back under the knob, she holstered the six-gun and looked at the helpless Cort stretched out on the bed.

He looked up at her as she came closer and held his gaze.

And in that look it was revealed that the doomed must love the most, the ache in their souls must be shared, the hopeless loneliness must be overcome and punished.

"Be sure of yourself," Cort said.

"I'm sure enough," she said, pulling off her shirt, coming close to the bed.

"The Mexicans have a saying—*Ni modo. . . .*" he said, staring up at her firm breasts. "It means there is no way out."

"I know another one," she said fiercely, slipping off her boots and pants. *"Vale pura madre,* and that means bullshit!"

As thunder boomed outside and shook the building, she leaned down to kiss him, but he struggled away and demanded, "Why are you doing this?"

Forcing him back on the mattress, she hooked his

handcuffs over the top of the bed and drew his pants down.

"Because tomorrow we might both be dead," she said, straddling him, lowering her body over his even as he struggled against her.

Bowing over him, her damp hair brushed his forehead and she kissed him as she wanted to.

His face hardened and he arched his back, setting himself.

"Promise me," she murmured as she lifted and settled, "promise you'll leave Herod for me."

"No," he murmured, just as she slammed him against the bed and their bodies joined in the explosion of fevered meeting, the clutch and release, the wrestling of sweating animals, the grappling swoon of little death.

KE-RACK! came the lightning bolt exploding outside.

"Promise," she sobbed, her teeth clamping into his cheek.

— 11 —

A ROOSTER WITH BONY SPURS GROWING FROM THE inside of his legs like pointed horns, crowed, stretching his neck and standing on his toes. His neck plumage stood out like a burnished golden bumbershoot, his red eyes bulged, and his challenge tore through the pale blue quietude of the town, announcing that he was king, boss stud, champion cock wherever his crow was heard.

Hardly had he settled back on his perch than from the other side of town came a similar yet more strident crow from a rooster with longer neck and larger spurs, and with more powerful wings to use as clubs, should the two roosters ever meet.

Other roosters joined the eloquent morning fray, asserting their authority, attempting to dominate their world by the length, breadth, and ferocity of their crowing.

That any of them would ever meet face-to-face was unlikely. Each rooster would guard his hens in a chicken house or barnyard, and the hens would stay close to their nests, so that for all the threatening blasts of supremacy assaulting each other around the town, nothing much would change.

As the sun rose, the roosters returned to strutting around the hens, treading them into the dust when they came close, and keeping a sharp eye out for grasshoppers.

Except for Ira's Worrisome Eats, the town was devoid of activity, because the outlaws and gunmen and their courtesans were not interested in a daily work routine and preferred to spend most of their waking hours in the night.

It was in the night that their gaudy clothes looked like hand-tailored finery and the bitter lines of their faces, their scars, their hard edges, were softened and made acceptable, while the women's painted masks were transformed to the bright features of an exuberant and flushed youth long gone.

Pausing before entering the small restaurant, she looked up at the big house and saw no sign of activity except for a single guard in his tan duster uniform standing on the front porch. Blackbirds picked through the street, owning it for the moment, and a gray cat futilely stalked them with his tail twitching and his eyes aglow, until a stray mongrel came out of the alleyway and sent both cat and birds flying.

Cats and dogs, she thought, pleased that the rain

was gone but not so pleased with the cats and dogs idea. It could rain cats and dogs, or people could fight like cats and dogs. Before dark the street would be a killing ground.

Inside, old Ira filled her coffee mug first, then set about making her breakfast.

"Last day, ain't it?" he asked over his shoulder. "For the quick-draw contest, I mean," he added apologetically.

"It's the day of reckoning." She nodded. "Who will win the money? Who will be dead meat on Charlie Moonlight's gut wagon?"

"Goin' to be a wedding right soon," Ira said, flipping hotcakes. "The Kid and Mattie Silk are goin' to tie the knot."

"Why?" she asked, smiling.

"Seems to me the Kid is trying to grow up faster'n his time. Wants it all right now. Wife, family, house, business, and headman, all at once."

"Suppose he gets it all? What would he do then?"

"Get bored and mean, I suppose, just like his dad," Ira said heavily, and put the plate of flapjacks, eggs, and sausage in front of her.

As she ate, he said lugubriously, "Not too many of you left, is there?" And answering his own question, said, "There's you and the preacher, the Kid and Herod . . . who else?"

"That's it. If the Kid's getting married, maybe he'll drop out for his honeymoon. And maybe the preacher will back off, and I can have Mr. Herod all to myself."

"That's crazy, lady!" the old man protested. "Better you ride out of this town and let somebody dry-gulch him when he ain't lookin'. It'll happen soon enough."

"I bet you've been saying that ever since he took over the town," she said quietly, pushing the empty plate away and finishing her coffee.

"But what's the matter with just stayin' alive?" he asked worriedly.

"It's different for me, Ira," she said. "I can't even start living until I kill that sonofabitch."

As she stood in the doorway, she saw that a long table had been set up in the middle of the street. A three-tier cake, bottles of champagne, and glasses sat waiting while a crowd gathered on the front porch of the saloon.

Someone had decorated the porch with chains of colored crepe paper and paper flowers, and a sheet covered the blind boy's shoeshine stand to make an altar.

Coming closer, she saw the Kid dressed in striped pants, a pleated white shirt with a sky-blue cravat, and a gray mourning coat, standing beside Mattie Silk, who was dressed all in pink-dotted Swiss, ribbons and bows, pink pearls and lace adorning the pink satin sheath. Tucked into her yellow hair was a sparkling tiara from which hung a pink veil. Behind Mattie stood four of her coworkers, all dressed in pink gowns.

Standing at the altar before them, still in chains, Cort finished reading from the Bible: "And whither thou goeth, I will go . . . where you dieth, will I die . . . if ought but death part thee and me . . ." Then, looking up at the couple, he solemnly said, "Kid, do you take this woman, Mattie Silk, to be your lawfully wedded wife?"

"I sure do," the Kid sang out, grinning.

"Do you, Mattie Silk, take this man, Kid Herod, to be your lawfully wedded husband?"

"Yes, yes, a thousand times yes!" she cried out.

"Then with the power vested in me I now pronounce you man and wife. Kid, you may kiss the bride."

The Kid lifted the pink net veil and kissed Mattie's cherry-red lips. The bridesmaids wept, the crowd whooped and hooted their congratulations.

The red-eyed bridesmaids threw handfuls of rice at the couple, and the Kid led Mattie out into the street.

As Horace uncorked the champagne, Mattie and the Kid together cut the first slice of cake.

Off to one side a small fat man played the accordion and the mongrel howled.

"Lady!" the Kid called to her. "Come give me a good luck kiss to send me off on!"

Coming close, she studied Mattie's young untroubled face, kissed her on the cheek and said, "All the best for you, Mattie."

Mattie blushed and said, "Gee, thanks, I just never thought it'd happen."

Turning to the Kid, she looked into his bright blue

eyes and was pleased to see no shadows of fear or sharp edges of desperation.

"Good luck, Kid," she said, and kissed his lips with a subtle sense of intimacy that came from being veterans of the gun.

Stepping back, she looked at him gravely, saw his eyes shift slightly over her shoulder, then return dark and brooding before he could cover up.

"What?" she asked.

"The old man," the Kid murmured, putting on his amiable, open smile again.

Turning slowly, she saw Herod sitting on his bench alone, watching and waiting. The small sneer on his wide mouth came across as a dare meant to provoke her, to frighten her, to rattle her nerves and force her to huddle down in the dust.

Courage, she thought. All it takes is the courage to face him.

Forcing herself to go slow, she strolled across the street directly to him. His face, shadowed by the tin canopy, was dark except for the cheekbones highlighted with crimson.

Her own features set hard with determination as she faced him and said succinctly, "I challenge you."

Leaning forward into the light, his face changed, seeming to sag like peach jelly, and he murmured in a small voice, "Go away."

"Don't put me off now," she said harshly, "I'm not fighting anybody else. I want YOU!"

Shaking his head slowly, his mind preoccupied by

a different problem, he looked off at the mountains and said, "I have already been challenged."

She stared at him in disbelief, but seeing the truth in his face, she turned back to Cort in the middle of the street and yelled, "You bastard, you promised!"

Cort looked at her, puzzled, and spread his manacled hands in a gesture of helplessness.

What the hell was going on? she asked herself with a sense of growing desperation. Had Cort challenged Herod or not?

Looking at the wedding party, she glanced over the faces until she saw the Kid looking back at her. He nodded sheepishly, winked, and said, "It's time for me to see if I'm my father's equal."

Her face registered the horror she felt, and the Kid tried to lessen the shock by saying, "I can handle it."

Shaking her head, she turned back to Herod. "You'd fight your own son?"

"You can't refuse a challenge. Those are the rules everyone understands. They're my rules, too," Herod said, still speaking as if she were somewhere along his distant gaze.

Anger flashed in her eyes and her body went rigid as she thought to draw and kill him in this instant before the horror could go farther.

"Don't try," Herod said bleakly, jerking his head at the uniformed men stationed on the rooftops, their carbines at the ready.

"Call off your guards. I'll count to three and we'll get it over with," she said, her hand hanging loosely by the walnut grips of her .44.

"I'm honored by the intensity of your ambition," Herod said, "but the contest is not being run by a frivolous woman, it is being run by me."

"I'm going to put a bullet in your head even if the Kid kills you first," she said fiercely, and turning away, she heard his taunting laugh and his mocking voice.

"But first you will abide by my rules . . ."

Crossing over to the saloon porch, she asked the blind boy, "Cort?"

"Inside on his chain." The boy nodded at the bat-wing doors.

She found Cort chained to the brass foot rail before the bar, watching Horace marking up his chalkboard.

She watched as he printed MR. HEROD VS THE KID NOON, and below, LADY VS CORT 6PM.

"What are we going to do?" she asked Cort, frowning. "We can't fight each other!"

"I know . . ." Cort said, shaking his head. "It's been his scheme all along . . . always a jump ahead of everybody else."

"I mean to kill Herod," she said flatly. "Nothing can change that."

"No, you can stand down and let me fight him in the final," Cort said. "What difference does it make who kills him?"

"Someday I'll tell you," she said, not changing her mind.

"If he's still alive after the finals, you can have your chance at him." Cort wanted to change her mind, but hearing the bat-wing doors swing open and the rattlesnake spurs crossing the dusty floor, he said, "Here comes the big he-boar."

"You said it right," Herod said strongly, "and the big he-boar says it loud and clear that you both are going to fight, nobody walks out of the contest now. Nobody's standing down."

"You don't tell me what to do!" she snarled, turning on him.

"Lady, if you even look like you're trying to leave town, my men will kill you deader'n a butchered whore," Herod said savagely, his broad shoulders bowing forward, his eyes bulging, his neck swelling. "If you refuse to fight Cort, my men will kill you both on the spot. You had your chance to quit and it's gone. In my town, women don't have the right to change their minds."

"It's not that I'm a woman that's bothering you," she came back at him, "it's because I can top you in a fair fight!"

"I promise you that after you kill Cort, you'll have a fair chance to back up your brag," Herod said, "meanwhile, it's getting along toward noon and I wouldn't want to disappoint the boy."

Leaving them, Herod walked back out into the street and saw that the table with the cake and champagne had been moved out of harm's way, and, checking the sun, decided its position overhead would not be a factor. Moving on down the street, he settled into his easy stance.

The clock said two minutes of twelve, but as she charged out into the street, she saw the minute hand click forward.

Going directly to the Kid, she hotly demanded, "What can you get out of this? What can you possibly win?"

The Kid frowned and thought about it for a moment. "I just want his respect."

She stared at him sadly and murmured, "It's so pitiful. . . ."

"I don't need no pity," the Kid snapped. "I'm his son, and if this is the only way to make him admit it, then put the blame on him."

Suddenly shifting into his arrogant, show-off role, he turned away and walked out into the middle of the street and made his monologue to the crowd as he strutted a small circle.

"The gunfight—I mean a first-class, blue ribbon gunfight—is in the head, not the hands. The only thing that makes him invincible is because you all think he is. Maybe five years ago he was pretty fast, but from then on he's been gettin' fatter and lazier and slower. Now he's riding his bluff. He's second best. And myself, would you believe it . . . ?"

Whipping his gleaming six-guns free, he spun them with dazzling skill, tossing them left and right like birch leaves in a wind, tossing and spinning freely, merrily.

"I'm just about the best there is in the whole world!"

Stopping where he started, the Kid sheathed his guns, gave Mattie a goofy grin, then settled himself to face Herod down the street.

The clock ground through its final seconds, and a hush hung over the street like a black veil.

Herod shifted his body to a more comfortable stance, slipped his black silk glove on, smoothed his coat down, and eyed the Kid steadily.

She wanted to scream and run out between them and cry out "No! This is wrong!" but she felt Cort's steadying hand touch hers.

The Kid held his grin, brushed a pebble aside with his boot, leaned forward intently, his bright blue eyes shining.

The clock rumbled and she heard the telltale tick.

Came the rasp of the gears and the minute hand jerked over, turning a pawl that in turn released a spring, and the clock chimed.

Hardly had the striker punched the chime than two shots simultaneously drowned it out. The crowd flinched and stared at the two men, who in a blink of an eye had drawn and fired, their six-guns still extended, the acrid odor of gun smoke filling the air.

Herod stood as always, tall, bull-shouldered, invincible.

The Kid stood stock-still, his gun extended, but his eyes were closed.

She saw the red, red rose bloom from his white pleated shirtfront and sucked in her breath.

Slowly his knees gave way, and she leaped into the

street to catch him. She didn't know why, but she knew he must not fall alone into the dirt.

His gun landed to one side and she caught his shoulders to break his fall.

Cradling his head on her knee, she murmured, "Easy there, Kid, easy does it. . . ."

Opening his eyes, he stared up at her, trying to focus the chaos of his thoughts.

"Did I get him?" he asked, his voice pleading anxiously.

"Yeah," she lied, "good as you could."

They both heard the rattlesnake whirr of spurs approaching, and the Kid bit his lip as the darkness came rolling in and the spiral began.

"Shit . . ." he groaned in disappointment, then beseeched her, "Please hold my hand, lady, I been alone so long. . . ."

She took his right hand and squeezed down hard.

"I'm here, Kid," she murmured. "I'm with you all the way."

He shook his head slightly, and as his eyes slowly closed, he muttered, "If you want to kill him, you've got to be faster than God."

His body twisted sideways and his throat gargled bright blood, and the life went out of him.

For a moment she wondered, Where did it go? Where did it go so quickly? Then she groaned with a sorrow that might have brought down a mountain. She heard Mattie Silk howl hysterically, and she laid the Kid's head down on his hat, brushed his hair back, and saw Doc Wallace bending down beside her, shaking his head.

As Doc Wallace moved back, Herod took his place and looked down at his son.

She tried to read whatever emotions he might have, and all she saw was uncertainty. Gazing down at his son's lifeless body, he couldn't make any sense of it. It wasn't a matter of right and wrong, it was a matter of making things orderly, but this was not orderly, could not be, because something was missing now. Could it be a part of himself? He was undecided, unable to put the pieces together in an orderly manner now that they had been changed.

She thought she saw a sense of impotent torment touch his grave features, a lostness that had never been there before.

"Your son, Mr. Herod."

"Maybe not . . ." He spoke, his voice husky. "If she was unfaithful once, why wouldn't she have been unfaithful before? It has to be one or the other, or you can't be sure. That's why they have to be killed—to keep things straight and know who belongs to who. He was more like a mechanic than like me, but only she ever knew for sure. . . .No, I don't think he was *my* son. . . ."

Staring down, he seemed to understand the point of his rambling, which was that there was no one he could trust. Not his wife nor his son, and perhaps not even himself.

"If she'd just done what she was supposed to do, none of this would have ever happened," he rambled on. "A woman must be true to her husband, otherwise you don't know what sort of mongrels are bearing your name. The first commandment should read: Thou shalt be true to your man or suffer death, because, if she breaks her vow, then you have to kill all the mongrels, otherwise all you've got from your manhood is chaos . . ."

"He looked just like you," she said cruelly.

"You witless slut," he said sharply, looking at her with eyes blazing, "in four and a half hours I'm going to have the pleasure of seeing you or that son of God lover of yours bleeding right here in my street!"

Stiffly, he walked past the silent crowd, striding on up the street toward his house.

Charlie Moonlight brought his cart up, and with the help of curious bystanders, the Kid's body was loaded aboard.

Mattie Silk tried to climb in after it, shrieking, howling her pain, but her bridesmaids held her back and Charlie Moonlight drove off toward the graveyard.

As the crowd drifted aimlessly away, with none of its usual elation, she walked catty-cornered across the street toward the Kid's gun shop.

A heavy sadness gripped her spirit, as if the Kid had been her own son or lover.

It's not really a matter of close relationship, she thought, it was more that he should have been a bright, busy, skylarking asset to the human race if he hadn't been cursed by his parenthood. Even then he'd done his best to share his brightness, his comedy and joy of life, as opposed to the dour, dank, decaying spirit of this tragic town.

Inside the gun store she felt a warmth of presence, as if he might be close by, but she knew it was not him, it was his way of doing things that still made the room alive. She looked over the bright posters, the polished weapons lining the walls, and thought sadly that the world of everyone was diminished.

Nothing had changed when Dred or Scars or Montoya or any of the other gunfighters had died, but the world rocked back for the worse when the Kid went over.

She looked at the framed, faded picture of the boy with the six-shooters in his hands and the bandoliers crossed over his bare chest, smiling proudly, like he'd learned how to become a man.

"Become a man! Fuck you, man, and fuck your guns that prop you up!" she snarled at the picture, and smashed it against the wall.

Without a hog handy to kick barefoot, she started to vent her anger on the pile of dynamite boxes where she'd once slept, and halted her boot in midair as she realized her error.

"Oh, hell . . ." she muttered. Sitting down on the makeshift bed, she put her face in her hands and put herself in the place of a small boy whose mother is gone and whose future depends upon knowing his father.

"What a shitty trick to play on little kids," she murmured aloud, pounding her fist in her hand monotonously, close to tears.

"Don't—" Cort said, coming through the door draped in chains.

Looking up, she asked bitterly, "Where's your keeper?"

"He's full of forty rod," Cort said. "The whole town's getting drunk. And not for fun. Killing the Kid took the devilment out of them, and now all they want to do is drown their sorrows."

"Sorrows?" she asked cynically.

"They're all sad and sentimental about when they were younger they were eager little rascals ready to take on the world and help out Ma and Pa, but then something changed their ways. . . ."

"Cort," she said suddenly, "the Kid was a locksmith, too. There's a thousand keys in that case."

Clanking past her to a case filled with door locks and padlocks, he fumbled with the lid, but his numbed fingers failed him.

"Let me . . ."

Opening the door, she picked out a batch of assorted keys wired together and started trying them one at a time on the handcuffs.

"We've got about four hours before we shoot each other," she muttered, seeking the right key. "You have any ideas?"

Herod took a hot bath and changed into a fresh suit of clothes, and as he performed his ablutions he explained to himself that he was downcast because for all the really splendid contests, the people didn't seem to be having much fun. They'd hardly applauded when he'd downed the Kid, and that had been very close. They just didn't appreciate the subtleties and refinements of the game, and the real beauty of the contests was wasted on the insensitive drunken rabble.

What none of them realized was that if the Kid had waited until next year, he might have won.

None of them realized that he was perfectly aware of the Kid's speed, that he'd goaded him into a challenge on this Jamboree instead of having to possibly lose on the next one.

The old fox doesn't miss any tricks, he thought, nodding to himself in the beveled-glass mirror.

The Kid knew he wasn't ready yet, but he had to do it anyway or lose face.

Too bad, Kid, he thought smugly. You should have guessed the old swamp fox was thinking way ahead of you.

As he let his mind admire its own generalship, he was able to regain the poise he'd lost in the street when that woman had racked him with her blunt comments. With new, more correct thinking, the Kid became something else, more like a standard gunfighter who'd bucked the tiger and lost. Somebody else. An ambitious outsider threatening his crown. A faceless hot gun, dangerous, meaning to kill, while the image of the Kid drifted off into shadows, not connected with violence or death, just a smiling youngster who wasn't around anymore.

Feeling refreshed, he walked down the street to the

Old Bank Saloon, nodding cheerily to surly, sore-headed gunfighters along the way.

Glancing up at the clock, he saw that it was already past five o'clock. The next contest, and the best, as far as he was concerned, would commence in about half an hour.

He expected the saloon to go quiet as he entered, and he was glad to see Cort shackled to the piano with Ratsy close by.

Flicking his eyes over the quiet room, he asked Ratsy, "Where's the nauch?"

"She's still in town," Ratsy said blearily. "I seen her talkin' to the doc just a little bit ago."

"And how is the son of God feeling now?" Herod asked Cort.

"A little better than the Prince of Darkness," Cort said.

"Ratsy, you going to stand for this infidel talking to me like that?" Herod asked.

"No, sir, I can't stand a smart mouth!" Ratsy threw a loop of chain over Cort's head that settled around his neck, then jerked him off the piano stool.

"Be careful, Ratsy, don't bang him up too much. I want him to be able to fight."

"I hate the sonofabitch!" Ratsy said drunkenly, and jerked on the chain again.

"Ratsy, pay attention or you might not be with us much longer," Herod said coldly. "I want him able to kill his sweetie."

12

NOT SUNSET OR MOONRISE, NOT NONES OR VESPERS, THE hour would be the common six postmeridian, which was called suppertime.

But supper would be late on the third day of the Jamboree.

The hour was reserved for the lady to kill Cort or Cort to kill the lady, the duel planned by the architect of death, John Herod, or planned by the fated lovers; no one, not even the blind boy, knew for sure.

All that was known on the street was that there would be a corpse at suppertime.

The clock hands stood almost opposite each other at one minute until six.

Horace the bartender made his announcement, and the whole town, including the most terrorized of townspeople, were gathered on the boardwalks, verandas, and balconies to watch, because this pair was different. Neither wanted to fight each other. Neither respected Mr. Herod. Both had proved to be fast and crack shots. Later on one of them might be good enough to kill off Herod.

Cort stepped out on the street near the town square where Herod's bench was located. The lady came out of Doc Wallace's office.

Cort was given the old rusty Colt and one cartridge, and he stood in the street disheveled and weary. He saw the three faceless sharpshooters stationed strategically on the roofs.

Herod, wearing a white brocade coat, settled on his bench and looked up at the clock.

The inner workings of the clock commenced their grinding and a smile of anticipation touched Herod's heavy features.

Came the telltale tick, the pause, and the hammer struck the bronze chime . . . ONE.

Neither drew nor even showed fight.

"Do it, lady!" Cort yelled. "It's nothing to me!"

TWO, the chime rang out. Herod's back straightened and his head pushed forward, scenting trouble.

"Go ahead, Cort!" she cried out as the chime hit THREE. "Get it over with!"

"Get on with it!" Herod roared. "A fair fight or you'll both die!"

FOUR bonged the clock, still neither made a move to draw.

"Dear love, you've got to do it. Go ahead, I deserve it," Cort said clearly.

"It's better you kill me, then you can kill Herod," she responded in a strange, defeated voice.

FIVE the clock chimed.

"On six both of you will draw and fire or be executed!" Herod roared, gesturing to the rooftop riflemen.

SIX clanged over the street, and both drew in unseen blurs, firing so quickly no one could ever swear to exactly what they saw. Hands flashing, fire and smoke blooming, and in that haze of bitter gun smoke, they saw her six-gun fall to the ground, her hand clutching at her breast, and the red staining her shirt and fingers.

Staring off at Cort, she stumbled forward and crumpled to the ground.

Doc Wallace hurried out from his doorway and knelt beside her.

After listening for a heartbeat, the doc shook his head sadly and glared at Cort. "You win, you rotten preacher. How does it feel?"

Cort let his pistol fall from his hand as his shoulders slumped. "Don't blame me—blame him," Cort said, nodding bleakly over at Herod.

"Nice shooting, Reverend." Herod chuckled, his face aglow with joy.

Charlie Moonlight and the close-by onlookers approached the lady's crumpled form, and 'Doc stood to his full height in rage and yelled, "Get away, you thieving bastards! You're not going to plunder this poor lady!"

Spreading his greatcoat over her, he crouched down on creaky knees and gently lifted her in his arms, glowered at the disappointed group, and carried her into his office, kicking the door shut with his heel.

Cort stood humbly, with no pleasure in his victory.

"You're a natural born killer, Cort," Herod said, eyeing him closely. "I knew it when you were just a snot-nosed kid. All I ever did was teach you the finer points."

Cort's massive hands clenched and his face trembled as his hatred for Herod built into a thundering tower of wrath.

Suddenly going berserk, Cort lunged toward Herod, but the uniformed guards intervened before he could get close enough to land a blow. As he struggled against the guards, Ratsy tried to lock the manacles to his wrist.

Cort viciously butted Ratsy in the face, crunching his already swollen nose, and Ratsy screamed in pain.

With three men holding him back, Cort still pushed forward to yell directly in Herod's face.

"You bastard! You'll burn in hell for this! You can't hide behind your hired guns forever!"

From behind, Ratsy clubbed him with his gun, sending him to his knees.

As Cort shook his head, trying to clear his mind, Ratsy snapped the handcuffs tightly around his wrists and ran the chain through the leg irons.

Glaring at Herod, Cort snapped, "Damn you, why don't you give me just half a chance at you!"

Herod grinned down at the helpless Cort and shook his head in mock disbelief. "Cort, you're always thinking the worst of me. Why is that? I raised you up from a half-starved pup into a well-to-do outlaw with a great future in front of you, but what do I get? I get a message my protégé has run off to Mexico. I bring him back and try to talk reason to him, and I get accusations of cowardice, that I'm hiding behind my hired hands. . . ."

"Nothing can save you, Herod. If it's not me, it'll be somebody else," Cort said fiercely.

"You're forgetting we haven't finished the Jamboree. You'll get your chance, Cort, and not because you say so, but because I say so. The rules must be obeyed, and the rules say tomorrow is the final day. I'll let you pick the time for me to kill you."

"Daybreak," Cort said, his face filled with deadly purpose, the serenity of the man of God replaced by a rage to kill.

"Let's call it six A.M. I'll see you then." Herod nodded and walked steadily back up the street to the big house, his guards fanning out, routinely taking their positions.

"C'mon," Ratsy muttered, jerking on the chain and leading his captive over to the Old Bank Saloon.

Passing the shoeshine stand, Cort heard the blind boy murmur, "I'm sorry, Mr. Cort."

Cort saw the boy's downcast features, and said huskily, "Keep your chin up, son. We're not done yet."

Before he could say more, Ratsy yanked on the chain and forced him to follow inside.

"Set," Ratsy commanded, shoved Cort into a chair at an empty table and went over to the bar. Returning with a bottle of forty rod, Ratsy slumped in the chair opposite Cort and poured himself a glass of the clear.

"You don't get any," Ratsy said, and gulped down half the glass. "You been nothin' but trouble ever since me'n Flat Nose brought you back."

"Don't blame it on me," Cort said. "I wasn't bothering anyone down there."

"You ruined my old pard." Ratsy frowned, finishing the glass and pouring more of the clear. "Old Flat Nose and me go back a long ways. Now his kids are out on the street."

"That was your boss's doing, not mine," Cort said quietly.

"You blew off his shoulder and now he's a cripple," Ratsy said sadly. "Him'n me, we shared out with each other ever since we joined up."

Lifting his glass, he said sadly, "Here's to my old partner Flat Nose, who never ever turned against a friend."

Again he drank, and said, "I'm feelin' better now."

"That stuff will rot your brain out," Cort said, his eyes flicking around the room crowded with raucous gunfighters making the most of the final night of the Jamboree.

"I got the best boss ever was. We're just closer'n pups in a basket. He says go burn out this preacher and bring him back, that's what I do."

"But what did you get out of it except a pat on the head, Ratsy? What does he pay you off with?"

"He finds me easy banks to rob," Ratsy said angrily. "That's what he does. I ain't had any trouble robbin' banks ever since we teamed up."

"And what's his cut, Ratsy?"

"Sixty-forty. I'm makin' more'n I ever did before, and I get to lay low here between tricks."

"And what does he charge for that?"

"None of your goddamned business!" Ratsy said angrily, lifting his glass unsteadily and managing to bump his nose.

"Damn it!" he cried out in pain, and gingerly touched the swollen beak with his index finger. "You broke it! Twice you broke it! And I been good to you, too. . . ."

"You should have stayed out of the way."

"An eye for an eye," Ratsy yelled. "A tooth for a tooth!"

"You better sleep it off, Ratsy." Cort frowned at the smaller man.

"You think you're so damned smart! I can tell you're up to something," Ratsy snarled, nerved up. "Put your hands on the table where I can see 'em."

Cort stared at him worriedly but didn't move.

Ratsy swung his fist at Cort's head, but Cort managed to dodge most of the blow.

"Steady on, Ratsy," Cort said as Ratsy stood and moved around behind him.

"I said hands on the table and you better mind me, mister!" Ratsy said in as hard a voice as he could muster, followed with his doubled-up fist hammering the back of Cort's neck.

Cort slowly brought his hands up and placed them on the table.

"Flat down!" Ratsy snarled.

"Ratsy, don't do something you might be sorry for later on." Cort flattened his hands out on the table, looking around the room futilely for help.

Still standing behind Cort, Ratsy pulled his heavy Colt from its holster, reversed it so that he was gripping the barrel, and muttered, "Break my nose once, maybe I could take that, but break my nose twice, no! Ratsy don't take that from nobody!"

On the last word he swung the butt of the Colt down on Cort's right hand so hard, Horace at the bar heard the bones crack a second before Cort screamed in agony.

In his office Herod lifted his head as if he'd heard the cry, listened a moment, and returned to studying the map of Arizona and New Mexico territories. Most of the towns within a radius of a hundred miles of Redemption were marked with a red ink cross, which meant their banks had already been robbed once. If there were two crosses, it had been robbed twice.

From all the cross-hatching in red, it was easy enough to see that the ground around Redemption had been pretty well covered.

He knew it was only a question of time before he moved his base of operations to a bigger town with more opportunities in the hinterland around it, but it had to be an orderly, planned shifting of forces. Maybe Prescott in the north . . . Likely it was far enough out of the way that, like Redemption, the Federals paid no attention to it.

I'm getting barn sour in this town, he thought. Life's too short to waste it being bored to death in a damn ghost town.

Maybe he should just give up this life and move over to Tucson and run for public office, become a patron of the arts, take over at the top instead of the bottom . . .

Still, he thought, I'd miss the killing.

Putting the map aside, he looked down the lantern-lighted street and saw the boardwalk crowded with people patiently waiting for dawn.

Damn fools, he thought. Why don't they go home and go to bed? Why wait all night to see a fight that would be over in two or three seconds?

You blink an eye, you'll miss it. He smiled down at the throngs of people.

Then he realized what they were waiting for and he laughed.

"You're wasting your time, you sonsabitches," he

said out loud. "I cannot lose that fight in any way, fashion, or form."

By the light of the lanterns, Horace lugged the Wells Fargo money box out to the veranda of the saloon and placed it across from the blind boy's shoeshine stand.

The boy sat morosely on the stand thinking about the lady and how wrong it was that she should be killed. It wasn't right. She'd been so confident the day before, and bought a block of phosphors, a pack of straight pins, a bottle of red ink and some peppermints, a ball of string, and a small pair of pliers, like she meant to go on living. Surely not like she was getting ready to die. It just didn't add up, he thought miserably, but then, nothing ever did for him. He'd known better than to let his guard down with her, but she'd treated him square and he missed her too much now.

With the clanking of chains, Ratsy dragged Cort out onto the veranda, and by the light of the hanging lanterns, he unlocked the manacles from around Cort's wrists.

After buckling the old Colt to Cort's waist, Ratsy glanced at the swollen right hand. "Better loosen that up, you're goin' to need it soon as the sun comes up."

"You shouldn't have done that, Ratsy," Cort said. "If I was you, I'd light a shuck out of this town and never come back."

"Sure . . ." Ratsy forced a smile despite a gut-sick

hangover. "Sure, you'd like me to run off and leave you loose."

"You don't have much time," Cort said, looking off to the east and seeing a faint blush touch the horizon.

"You don't scare me none," Ratsy said defiantly.

"Good morning, Doc," Cort said as the tall bearded man stopped on the boardwalk. "About time?"

"Another eight minutes," the doctor said, looking up at the town clock.

"Reckon you could bind up my hand some?"

The doctor came up the steps and examined the hand, probing gently with his finger. "Looks like Ratsy's work," he muttered into his beard. "I can bandage it so you can use a couple fingers, but you'll never get that hand around the butt of a gun again."

Cort shrugged. "Anything will help."

Opening his bag, the doc found a roll of cotton bandage and commenced binding up the hand.

"Too bad, Ratsy," the doc said, looking over at the small mouse-faced man. "You should have remembered how much Mr. Herod enjoys killing people in what he calls a fair fight."

"What are you sayin'?" Ratsy asked nervously.

"For all the evil in your boss, Ratsy, he gets great pleasure from killing a man who has at least a chance of winning. You've taken away the champagne and cherry pie and left him cold boiled potatoes."

Strolling down the street, Herod smiled coldly at

the townspeople, and in the hazy blue light of dawn, he saw that the town clock said five minutes till six.

Seeing the doc working over Cort's hand, he stepped up to the veranda where the blind boy and that young piece, Katie, waited amongst clustered gunfighters and townsfolk.

He relished the dreadful fear on their faces.

"What's the problem?" he asked, frowning as he saw the doc carefully wrapping the ruined hand.

"He looked like he was goin' to try somethin'," Ratsy said defensively. "Besides, he broke my nose again."

"Ratsy," Herod frowned and sighed, "you have twenty seconds to leave town."

"Wait, Mr. Herod!" Ratsy protested. "That ain't fair. You told me 'guard the prisoner' and I did!"

"You now have fifteen seconds," Herod said quietly.

Ratsy gawked at Herod's fixed features, groaned miserably, scuttled down into the street and ran off in the direction of the river.

"What shall we do, Cort?" Herod asked sympathetically. "We can't postpone it."

"No," Cort said, "we can't postpone it."

"There's all these people wanting to see you shoot me for entertainment. Suppose I draw with my left hand the same as you? I can kill with either hand, Cort. Can you?"

Cort didn't answer. Herod flexed his left and said, "I'm keyed up for a killing. I love the sensation.

There's no other exciting pleasure like it." Looking down the street he saw Ratsy sprinting, almost a speck in the distance. "Time's up, Ratsy."

Herod palmed his left hand Colt, and with only a sidewise glance, fired.

The bullet caught Ratsy at the base of the neck and lifted him off his feet. His body arced forward like a frog jumping, and he plunged head first into the dirt.

Knowing him, none of the thieves thought it worthwhile to walk that far to plunder his corpse.

"I've always wanted to fight you face-to-face, one on one, Cort," Herod said pleasantly. "Ever since I first saw you paunch that old banker who was blazing away at you with his buffalo rifle, I've wondered what it would be like to meet someone as unafraid as I am."

"Save it, Herod."

"I'll finish, if you please," Herod said with a steely voice, playing to the crowd. "It's been like a romance, in a way. It's been like ... like an itch I couldn't scratch."

Cort glanced up at the clock. "A minute to go . . ." and he started off down the street.

Herod stepped into the street and spoke quietly to a guard in a tan duster carrying a Winchester carbine. "Whatever happens, if I miss, kill him."

"Yes sir." The man nodded. "I'll pass the word."

As Cort reached his position in the street, he practiced drawing the Colt from the left-handed scabbard, then he thought, It didn't make any difference.

Scanning the rooftops, he saw the carbines poised in the hands of the guards, all set to whip to the shoulder, aim and fire.

Either way, he was dead.

Herod stopped, turned, his heavy bull shoulders bulging forward, his protruding eyes afire with joy.

Cort stopped and turned, knowing all hell would break loose any second.

He heard the groanings to the clockworks and set himself. He heard the telltale tick, but with the first sound of the chime—KA-BLOOY!—a horrendous explosion shook the street and the clock burst outward like a great bomb, sending raw splinters and fragments raining down on the street.

As Cort dived to the ground—BOOM!—the street rocked again and the upper floor of the saloon lifted and exploded, sending debris flying over the town.

Herod stood stock-still, stunned but unafraid. Looking down the street, he could no longer see Cort in the smoke and he felt vulnerable. Moving closer to the firehouse, he yelled, "What the hell is going on!"

Before there could be an answer—BA-ROOM!— the front of the old Stockman's Rest blasted off into the street, leaving the open rooms intact and naked women dashing to the rear landing.

Herod's three councillors shifted their carbines this way and that, seeking a target, but there was nothing but falling debris, smoke, and dust.

Herod used the bench to shield himself from flying brick fragments, and after a lull, rising in awesome rage, he was immediately knocked to his knees by his own house going up in splinters, rock fragments and pulverized stone.

—K-R-R-RUMP! The two brick wings and the upper floor unfolded and blasted skyward with a concussion that shook down Abe's Harness Shop and the Lady's Wear.

As the cloud of dust settled, he rose slowly to his feet again. Blood ran from his nose and one ear. Looking up, he saw his three guards coming down from what roofs remained, still ready.

Through the turmoil, dust, and smoke, he saw a figure moving toward him from the other end of the street and thought it must be Cort coming at him.

Stock-still, he watched and waited as the figure stepped forward a slow pace at a time.

"That you, Cort?" he called. But there was no answer.

He shook his head to rid it of the ringing, but he didn't step back.

Backlighted by the rising sun, the figure came toward him like a ghost, and then he saw her white face through the dust and cried out, "You're dead!"

As she came closer, he saw the red stain on her blouse.

He couldn't believe it, nor comprehend it. Frozen in inaction, he tried to put the parts together so they were orderly and made sense, but this apparition was not sensible nor orderly. It simply could not be, yet she came on.

He realized suddenly that he had been tricked and

had lost the advantage, but he didn't know how or why.

"WHAT ARE YOU? WHO ARE YOU?" he screamed.

Thirty feet away from him, she stopped, reached into her breast pocket, took out her father's remembrance and lofted it, spinning like a throwing star, to land between his feet.

Herod stared at the marshal's badge, the points straightened out, the gold and silver polished to their former glory.

Dumbly Herod looked up from the badge to her face, studying it, seeking to absorb it into his memory and connect it to a forgotten moment in his past.

Thunder. From across the river thunder came rolling, the sky was clear as a bluebird's eye, the day was fair, yet the thunder came rolling on. . . . Morning sunbeams warmed the street and larks sang. And the rumbling thunder of horse's hooves drummed up the river bluff like Jehovah's wrath, condemning and crushing the sweet green grass of home. . . .

Looking into her piercing eyes, he remembered their shape and expression of steady concentration.

—There's your poor daddy, he's goin' to be hung unless someone helps him out. Understand, little girl . . . ? Now listen to me, honey-punkin child—I'm goin' to give you a chance to set your daddy free. All you got to do is shoot that rope—and I'll set him loose. Can you do that—

As Herod held his poker face, he recalled the moment the child had shot her father as a peak of rapture, legendary in its naked evil, a cherished moment he would never regret.

In spite of the smoke and fine debris floating around, and the money box burst open, nobody in the street moved.

"You stole my life," she said. "I want it back."

While one guard still remained perched on the false front of the mercantile, another dropped to the ground next to the Kid's gun shop, and the other took a position behind a fifty-gallon water barrel in front of the barbershop.

As the man behind the water barrel took aim at her, Cort appeared behind him and struck him on the side of the head with the Colt in his left hand and seized the carbine.

As the other two guards shifted their aim to Cort, Cort fired the carbine, dropping the man by the gun shop, and at the same time he fired the Colt with his left hand. The guard's Winchester tumbled down over the tin canopy of the mercantile, followed a moment later by his groaning, caroming body crashing to the ground.

Scanning the street and the rooftops, Cort stood with the carbine's stock set against his hip and the Colt in his left hand, ready.

Seeing no hostile movements, he crossed on an angle and said clearly to her as well as Herod, "Now it's fair."

She looked at him, then at Herod.

"One on one," she said quietly.

Herod looked over his shoulder, hoping to see

some support, but all he saw was Cort in control of the street. Chewing on his lip, he wondered why there was no one to back him up, then he realized most of those still alive wanted him dead.

Not that it made any difference. He could still draw and fire faster and straighter than anyone anywhere. It just needed doing.

"You're not fast enough for me," he said, to spook her and gain the slight advantage.

"I am now," she said, "because I want my life back."

Herod's hand twitched, and through the hazy quietude came Katie's encouraging voice. "You can do it, miss. We all want our lives back."

Hoping that voice would distract her further, Herod's hand struck, clawed, pulled, leveled, and fired in one invisible flash.

She screamed as her own shot found its mark.

Hunching over and pressing the six-gun against her bleeding shoulder, she watched Herod take a slow step backward, stagger, then settle to his knees, bright arterial blood pumping from his left armpit.

His golden gun dragged a furrow in the dirt.

She lunged forward, not finished, and kicked the golden gun away. Holding her .44 a foot away from his broad forehead, she said, "I've been working on my aim since I was a little girl."

Thumbing the hammer back, she laid the muzzle between his eyebrows.

"Don't," Cort said, standing beside her. "Murder is different than kill or be killed."

"But we're both beyond redemption." She frowned. "What's the difference?"

"Nobody's ever beyond redemption," Cort said. "We just have to change our ways. Just have to stop the killing. We have to make life worthy of us."

"Life . . ." she murmured sadly, tears brimming in her eyes. "Oh, pity poor life."

"No," Cort said, "life is for rejoicing, there's still time for us."

She lowered the .44 and saw Herod sway and his eyes close, and realized her one shot had been enough for him and for her.

As Herod slumped to the ground, she muttered, "That dog meat's not even worth wrapping up."

Crawling toward Doc Wallace, Herod stared up at the old man and said beseechingly, "Help me . . ."

"I wouldn't piss on you if you was on fire," the old man growled, stepping back.

Looking up toward the front porch of the saloon, Herod groaned, "Help me—"

Crawling through broken bricks, dust, and Wells Fargo bills caught in the breeze, he begged, "Help me . . . Somebody . . . Take all the money . . . please . . ."

He was swimming slowly across the street, his hands dragging him through the dirt, trailing a rope of blood, his legs thrusting forward with a toad's pushing action. He saw the glimmer of his golden Colt just ahead like a mirage to a dying man's thirst in the desert. If he could just reach it . . . What would he do with it? he wondered. Everything should be in its place and all the pieces be in order . . . if he could grip the golden gun again, what next? What following piece of action? Who would he shoot? Everybody . . .

Everybody.

With the glimmer of gold in his eyes, Herod stretched out his hands and touched the gold and silver badge lying in the dirt. Bitterly his eyes closed, and in one last protest, as if he were seeing the gates of hell opening, he screamed, "NO!"

She felt the dizziness of shock and staggered, veering toward the ground until Cort caught her and held her erect.

"I want that badge," she muttered.

Katie ran down the steps, took the badge from Herod's twitching fingers and gave it to her.

Surrounded by outlaws and townsfolk grabbing at the loose Wells Fargo money, and half supported by Cort's good hand, she fired her Colt in the air.

As the mob fearfully turned to stare, she declared harshly, "Put away your guns and leave the money be! Anybody with a bounty on their heads has three minutes to ride out, starting right now!"

The wanted ones moved away, veterans of the owlhoot trail, but the townsfolk stared at her, not understanding, not knowing what to do anymore.

Standing tall, she held up the gleaming badge and said clearly, "Let's start over. The law's come back to town."

About the Author

Big Sur Writer

Writing Westerns

by Jim Cole

The Coast Weekly

Jack Curtis just had to wind up writing Westerns. One grandfather, his favorite, ran a saloon in a dusty cowboy town in western Kansas and had met Jesse James. Rumor had it he may have shot a man.

"Being an average boy," Curtis said, "I was enamored with this stuff a lot more than by my other grandfather—who was a straight, up-and-coming cattleman." Those extremes—the gunslinging ne'er-do-well and the honest owner of a 1000-acre ranch—produced Curtis.

Most of the year Curtis and his wife, LaVonn, can be found either at their Apple Pie Ranch in Big Sur, or in San Juan Bautista, where he works in a humble two-bedroom house, a photo of his mustachioed grandfather ("my no-good grandfather," Curtis said) watching him.

Like so many Midwestern farmers, the Curtis family was driven from the land in the 1930s. "I'm a Dust Bowler," Curtis said in an interview in San Juan Bautista. "Not exactly the Joad family, but close enough. My father lost everything. I believe he stole the car we drove west in."

In 1961, director Sam Peckinpah, a high school friend, offered him a job as a Hollywood scriptwriter. For twelve years he worked for Hollywood writing for a batch of popular shows, including *Have Gun Will Travel, Wagon Train, The Rifleman,* and *Zane Grey Theater.* In addition, he wrote for *Doctor Kildare, The Corrupters* and *Ben Casey.*

Six years ago an agent asked him if he had any Westerns. His response was not surprising. "I'm a tural Western writer. I want to get the poetry, to get humor, I want to get the music," he said.

Above Curtis's desk is a century-old photo of a mustachioed fellow wearing a wide necktie and a jacket. He has the steely gaze of a man who could very well have shot somebody and will watch over his grandson trying to write about it a century later.

About the Screenwriter

Screenwriter Simon Moore is a London resident who had never been in the American West until he visited director Sam Raimi and company on *The Quick and the Dead* location outside Tucson, Arizona.

Moore gained recognition as writer and director of a much-admired 1991 film titled *Under Suspicion*. Starring Liam Neeson and Laura San Giacomo, the suspense-drama was set in the late 1950s and concerned a seedy British private eye who became the prime suspect in his wife's murder.

In 1989, Moore wrote *Traffik*, a six-part serial about the international heroin trade directed by Alastair Reid. It aired on PBS in the United States, where the series won an International Emmy. The drama won many other awards as well, including England's BAFTA for best series, Broadcasting Press Guild's best series award, and three FIPA awards at the Cannes Film Festival. Moore also wrote the cult drama-comedy series *Inside Out* for the BBC in 1985.

Moore has had several plays produced in London's

West End, the most recent being his 1992 adaptation of Stephen King's *Misery,* which he directed with Sharon Gless in the lead role. In 1988 he co-wrote and directed *Up on the Roof,* an a cappella musical that earned three prestigious Olivier Award nominations in England and has been performed around the world.